HELLBEAST OF MARS

KIT KANE

Published worldwide
by
Seven Monsters Media Ltd.

Cover Design by MiblArt
miblart.com

Cannonball Express logo by John Barrie

All Media Rights Enquiries:
Micheline Steinberg Associates
info@steinplays.com

ISBN: 978-1-9998750-6-0 (Hardcover)
ISBN: 978-1-9998750-2-2 (Paperback)

For Phoebe

Contents

1

Hellbeast of Mars

"Horror beyond imagination! Savagery beyond belief!" The show-woman's voice rang with a strident theatrical doom, sending audible ripples of fear through her wide-eyed audience. "These and more are what await you here tonight, ladies and gentlemen. These and *much* more," upon which, almost as if on cue, an ear-shattering crash of thunder shook the air, and the interior of the dimly lit show tent flashed into shocking high-contrast, its heavy canvas no match for the Martian lightning storm raging outside.

In the front row of the packed tent, fifteen-year-old Laura Benton took a deep breath and attempted to rein in her pounding heart. *All just crowd-baiting nonsense,* she told herself. *The usual traveling show hokum…* and then felt her sweaty fingers close tighter around Billy's hand anyway. Dang it all, why couldn't they have gone to see a movie? Laura hated these kind of shows. Truly *hated* them. Then again, not like she'd really had any choice in the matter, right? When Billy Stibbs had *finally* plucked up the courage to ask her out and then suggested they come here, what was she gonna do? Start quibbling? Cos *dang it all* the boy was cute.

Turning Laura's way, Billy flicked his famously floppy fringe clear of his famously puppy dog eyes and flashed her a smile that could melt entire polar regions. Yeah, okay, Laura thought. Maybe she *could* put up with this hokum just a *little* longer…

As the last of the lightning faded and the tent flickered back into its carefully stage-managed dimness, the show-woman in the single spotlight—a towering, chisel-jawed lady; all knowing smile and gents' evening wear— resumed her melodramatic spiel:

"One last time then, folks, I urge you most sincerely, if you have a weak heart, please exit the tent now. Coronary failure is, I regret to say, not an uncommon reaction upon encountering the sight you are about to see. The *creature* you are about to meet," with which words the woman gestured to the object she stood beside—a three-meter-tall cubic affair hidden beneath a heavy canvas cloth. Adorning the cloth on all sides were lurid paintings of terror-stricken faces, each one directing its exaggerated horror at a huge blood-red question mark that dominated the section of the cloth facing the audience.

With the show-woman's gesture, a further murmur of fear swept through the crowd, and Laura felt Billy's left arm slip around her shoulder. Smiling to herself, she edged into it just the tiniest fraction.

"Many have tried to explain the anomaly I am about to present to you," the woman continued, her voice dropping low, drawing her audience in, "but they have tried in vain. Genetic experiment gone wrong? Radiation-spawned mutation? Alien killing machine? No one knows for sure. Most likely, no one ever shall. Of one thing only am I, personally, very certain: that coursing through the bloodstream of this, our diabolical captive, is nothing less than pure evil." The show-woman let the word *evil* hang there alone in the darkness for several torturous moments, then, with a blood-chilling gravity, began to reach for a corner of the painted cloth. Even as her fingers extended, another crash of thunder shook the air, still more murmurs of fear surging through the crowd, and when both sounds had faded to silence once more, the woman raised a single, teasing eyebrow, hand still outstretched, riding the suspenseful pause.

Laura had to admit it: hokum or not, the lady was good. *Danged* good. But then, the lady in question *was* apparently Zora Petrovna herself, and *Petrovna's Carnival of Mars* did have one almighty planetwide reputation to maintain.

With her fingers closing at last around a fistful of the painted drape, the show-woman's voice rose again to its full theatrical magnificence:

"Ladies and gentlemen," she boomed…

Here it came, Laura thought, gripping Billy's hand tighter still…

"May I offer you the horror sensation of the western quadrant…"

From offstage, a growl of timpani joined the rumble of rain-on-canvas…

"The terror of the entire Red Planet…"

Deep dissonant brass welled up now too, not so much music as an orchestrated moan of terror…

"The one, the only…"

A cacophonous, screeching fanfare…

"Hellbeast of Mars!"

And with an elaborate stage flourish, the woman whipped away the cloth from the three-meter-tall cubic object to reveal…

… a cage.

An *empty* cage.

An empty cage with its single rear door hanging

wide open.

The show-woman seemed to freeze where she stood, her eyes starting in shock. More than half the audience gasped in terror and shot to their feet, Laura among them, one hand clamped to her mouth to stifle her own cry of fear.

But then Laura noticed Billy, still seated beside her, entirely unperturbed, the last of an amused eyeroll just departing his oh-so-pretty features. Glancing up at her, Billy reached out and took Laura's hand again, giving it the gentlest of tugs to get her to sit back down.

Dang it all, Laura thought, kicking herself for being so pathetically hokum-susceptible, then firing an eyeroll of her own at the still amused Billy. *Yeah, okay, she got me.*

As she dropped into her seat once more, Billy leaned over, the end of that famously floppy fringe tickling Laura's ear. "Relax," the boy whispered. "All part of the—"

Then a blur of gray came slamming in from nowhere, and Billy was gone.

Just... *gone.*

That was when the screaming began.

The screaming and the *running.* Everyone. Racing for the tent's exit. A frantic, tumbling mass of horrified humanity, bolting, it seemed, for their very lives.

"Billy?" Laura managed to croak. Then a yell—

"BILLY!"—as someone, not Billy, grabbed her arm to pull her into the shrieking, escaping mob. Grabbed her *bloodstained* arm, some distant part of Laura's shock-numbed brain noted.

Because there was blood *everywhere.*

Blood *all over her.*

Billy's blood?

How…?

And then she was lost in the screaming throng, shoved and battered, carried along in the heaving crush till she tumbled from the show tent's entrance and went sprawling to the muddy ground outside. As yelling figures stampeded past, Laura fought to drag herself upright in the chaos, lightning as wide as the horizon tearing apart the sky above her, the traveling show's garish signs and placards strobing themselves into Laura's reeling mind:

TERROR BEYOND IMAGINATION!
SAVAGERY BEYOND BELIEF!
THE HORRIFYING HELLBEAST OF MARS!

As rain pounded the ground all around, yet more screaming crowds came pouring out of the show-tent, while from inside it, Laura heard something else now. Something that cut through the screams and the thunder like claws down a blackboard. It was a kind of shrieking animal howl, like nothing Laura had ever heard before.

Hauling herself to her feet, heart pounding in terror, Laura fought her way back to the tent's entrance. "BILLY!" she yelled again. But even as she stumbled up to the doorway, there came from inside the tent a loud crack of splintering wood, and all at once the entire huge canvas collapsed in on itself, a mass of twisting and writhing shapes revealed beneath it as its rain-sodden weight sagged down onto the many who had not yet managed to escape.

Then that shrieking animal howl rose up once more, and a further flash of sky-wide lightning revealed *another* form beneath the sagging canvas—something that whirled and thrashed and battered at the shapes around it with a relentless, devastating fury.

"Billy!" Laura managed one final time, before a mob of fleeing carnival goers rammed hard into her, and all was darkness.

2

Two Left Feet

"Ow!" Jess yelped.

"Sorry…"

"Ow *ow!*"

"Yeah, um, sorry…"

"Also, and this really does bear repeating, *ow!*"

Glancing down at the comfy low heels she had selected for tonight's dance, then at the hefty size ten currently removing itself from her mashed right foot, Jess Flint gave vent to a good-humored sigh, her mouth twitching into that wry but not unkind smile it often seemed to assume when faced with the fella before her. "Seriously, Dave, tootsies taking a major hit here. General principle, okay: on any given beat, your feet go where mine *aren't*."

"Gotcha," her frowning dance partner replied, and marshalling himself once more, the ever determined Dave from Staines stepped back into Jess's arms, then made another valiant attempt to lead off… mashing one fewer of Jess's toes this time round, an impartial observer might point out. So yeah, progress. Maybe. Of a sort.

As Jess and Dave lumbered their way around the tiny dancefloor of the Lucky Horseshoe Saloon, hordes of other dancing couples pressed in on them from every direction, the bar packed to bursting tonight as the four-piece jazz combo in the corner kicked out the kind of rhythm almost anyone could shake a leg to.

Or crush foot flesh to.

As was one's preference.

But even while enduring this fresh bout of toe torture, Jess found her smile only marginally diminished, it being a universally recognized fact that Mars's pre-eminent torturer of toes was someone with whom it was nearly impossible to get annoyed. Because all things considered, Dave Hart truly was the sweetest of fellas—one whom, if Jess were being honest, she could not now imagine her days here on the Martian frontier without. Smart, hardworking, funny (if you appreciated deeply obscure references to ancient sci-fi characters), the guy had proven himself time and again to be a genuine asset to Trans-Mars Haulage, the rail company Jess and her friends had started up a mere three short months ago. And not just because he made the finest java this side of, well, Java. Guy was shaping up to be a pretty decent engineer too. Okay, so in other ways their sci-fi-geek-in-residence might not always be the most switched on of Martian frontiersmen, but hey, considering he *was* actually from twenty-first century Earth and had essentially been defrosted from some kind of weird alien cryo-stasis those same three short months ago, the fella seemed to be coping pretty darned well with everything a twenty-*fifth* century red planet could throw at him.

Everything, it seemed, except dancing.

"How goes it, babe?" a voice from behind them inquired, Jess recognizing it immediately as the soft, throaty tones of her best friend and business partner Sally Chu. One brief jazzy beat later, knockout glamorous as ever in something black, slinky, and barely decent, the gal herself quickstepped into Jess's view, wrapped in the eager arms of some poor entranced young swain.

"Surviving?" Sally asked Jess.

"From the ankles up, sure," Jess replied, prompting a knowing grin from Sal.

"Gotcha. Little piggies wishing they really had

stayed at home, huh?"

As Jess laughed, Dave seemed to sag a little in her arms, before pausing mid-mash and then drawing back a step to frown at Jess and Sal. "Maybe I should go get us some drinks," he said.

"Good plan," Jess answered, unable to stop herself from adding, "Numb the pain."

The quip elicited a further snort of laughter from Sal, and frown deepening, Dave opened his mouth as if to say something more... but then seemed to think better of it and just shuffled off towards the crowded bar.

"Better make *hers* a double," Sally called after him.

"You pair *really* have to stop that," a new voice at Jess's shoulder put in, this one betraying the smooth English inflections of Jess's *other* best friend and business partner, Vera Middleton.

Uh-oh, Jess found herself thinking as she turned and took in the demeanor of the gal in question. Because Vera, peering at Jess and Sal over the rims of her librarian-esque half-moon spectacles, did not present the aspect of a happy bunny.

"Huh?" Sally said. "Stop what?"

"Making fun of Dave's dancing."

"What?" Jess said. "Oh, come on, Vera. It's just Dave."

"Yeah," Sally drawled. "Friendly banter. Dave knows that," and scooping Entranced Young Swain

11

up into her arms once more, Sally quickstepped her way back into the crowd, leaving Jess alone to face a not remotely mollified Vera.

With her school-ma'am-ish frown darkening, Vera raised her arms, took Jess into hold, and led her back onto the crush of the dancefloor, talking low as the pair of them stepped their way around the bustling room.

"You really don't see it, do you?" Vera said.

"See what?"

"*Dave.* He *likes* you."

"Huh? Oh, come on, Vera, that's ridiculous. It's *Dave.*"

Pushing her glasses back up onto her nose a fraction, Vera sighed. "You honestly have no idea how that sounds, do you?"

"Vera, get real. I say again, it's *Dave.* He likes… comics and science fiction and—"

"He is *also,* as far as one can ever be certain of such things, the owner of a fully functioning male winky, as well as, if I may say so, a rather sweet smile. Which, I cannot help but note, he is inclined to flash *your* way at regular intervals. The smile, that is, not the winky."

Jess took a moment to study her (oh-so) English friend. "Okay, first off, *winky?* Seriously? We will *absolutely* be revisiting *that* later. But back on topic, Vera, you're imagining things. *Regular intervals?* Dave does not smile at me at anything like *regular intervals,*" and with the intention of ramming home this clearly inarguable point, Jess turned to the bar to indicate the fella himself…

… only to find the uncooperative lummox smiling right back at her. *Sweetly*, goddammit.

"Okay, so he's a smiley geek," Jess blustered. "That doesn't prove—"

But then, for the third time in as many minutes, an unexpected voice joined the conversation from over Jess's shoulder. *This* voice though was one entirely unknown to her.

"Excuse me," it said. "I'm so sorry to bother you ladies, but would either of you by any chance happen to be Ms. Jessica Flint of Trans-Mars Haulage?"

Pausing in their dance, Jess and Vera turned as one to find a small, elderly woman peering up at them. Silver-haired, soft of feature, and dressed far too well for the spit-n-sawdust surroundings of the Lucky Horseshoe, the stranger stood there on the edge of the grimy dancefloor, all French lace and crinoline, as out of place as a tiara on a trash heap.

But while the old lady's apparel might have been the first thing Jess noticed about her, it was something else that captured Jess's full attention: the unmistakable glisten of tears, brimming in the woman's rheumy eyes.

"Um, yes," Jess replied, "I'm Jess Flint. Can I

help you?"

Drawing a lace handkerchief from her sleeve, the old lady dabbed at her eyes and said, "I hope you can, Ms. Flint. I surely do hope you can…"

3

Miss Lacey

"Here, let me top you up," Abby Flint said, hoisting the guest teapot from its trivet by the glowing hearth and approaching the elderly lady with it. Seated opposite, Jess watched her mom pour out another cup for their visitor, the momentary quiet affording Jess an opportunity to study this puzzling prospective client. By the flickering light of the parlor fire, Miss Lacey—the woman's name, Jess knew by now—looked no less prim and overdressed here in the modest surroundings of the Flint family's four-room frontier cabin than she had half an hour ago in the Lucky Horseshoe. She looked no less tearful either, though a gracious smile did tug at her lips as she said to Jess's mom, "Thank you, dear, you're very kind," raising the fine china cup to sip at her refreshed brew.

Eventually, Miss Lacey lifted her eyes again to Jess. "You still seem… unsure, Ms. Flint. If it's about the money—"

"No," Jess said, "it's not the money, it's just… You *really* can't find a scheduled passenger service to take you?"

"Not one that would get us there in time, no. And a stagecoach, I fear, would be slower still."

"Sure, but… chartering an entire train? Just for *yourself?*"

"And my sister, Ms. Flint. We come as a pair, Sissy and I. Always have done, always will."

Jess returned an understanding nod, while failing still to erase entirely the lingering frown that creased her brow. It wasn't that she couldn't do with the money. Business for Trans-Mars Haulage, while gratifyingly steady, couldn't exactly be described as booming quite yet, and the high-end oxygen breather units Jess's mom needed to keep her worsening asthma at bay weren't getting any cheaper. Quite the opposite, in fact.

As if reading Jess's thoughts, Abby Flint pulled her current breather from the front pocket of her apron and took from it as discreet a drag as she was able in the tiny parlor. The action itself was small, almost mundane, and a regular enough occurrence in the Flint household to be all but invisible under normal circumstances. Right now though, it was an unwelcome reminder that the atmosphere the local air barons saw fit to supply to the residents of Tranquility and its environs did not come even *close* to meeting the legal requirements for breathability. How they got away with such blatant flouting of the regulations, Jess could not say. And as for the air tax itself? Rising almost every month, *despite* the ever declining air quality. It wasn't like they had any kind of choice in the matter either. Ultimately, it was pay up or out you went to the Free Zones, where unpredictable pockets of *entirely* untreated and potentially poisonous atmosphere would take their toll on even the healthiest of lungs, let alone the kind of asthma-ravaged ones Jess's mom had to battle on with.

All things considered then, this hire was, on the face of it, a highly welcome and more than generous payout for very little effort on the part of Trans-Mars Haulage.

So why did Jess still feel reticent?

"Ms. Flint, I understand your concerns, truly I do," the old lady said, "but please be assured, my late husband left us well taken care of. The fee is not an issue here. The only real question is whether you, widely hailed as the fastest rail operator in the western quadrant, might be willing to take two elderly sisters to New Dakota in time to say a final farewell to their beloved mother."

From the determined look in the woman's eye, it was clear to Jess that Miss Lacey would have continued to expand upon this heartfelt plea, except that bubbling under the last of her words was a throaty, choked sound that stopped her. One uncomfortable pause later, the old lady again drew a hanky from her sleeve to dab at her brimming eyes.

Jess felt her heart give a lurch, and a sharp pang of guilt followed. Guilt for even *considering* turning away this soul in need. Cos let's face it. Injured wildlife? Lost children? Little old ladies who wanted to visit dying relatives in far flung regions of Mars? If they needed help, needed support, were hurting in any way at all, Jess Flint, as history had proven, was never *really* gonna say no to them, now was she?

"Miss Lacey, I…" Jess stammered, "… Okay, sure. Yes. We can do that. No problem. Consider us hired."

"Oh, *thank you,* Ms. Flint. Thank you *so much.* Now, if you'll excuse me, I really must get back to Sissy. She'll be anxious to know how I got on."

"Of course," Jess said, she and Miss Lacey rising together from their chairs while Jess's mom fetched the old lady's shawl from a hook by the hall door.

Mustering a smile, Jess approached Trans-Mars-Haulage's newest client and presented her hand, which the old lady, smiling now too, shook with an admirably businesslike firmness.

"So," Jess said, "if you and your sister can make your way to TMH for about midday tomorrow, that would be great. We *are* gonna need most of the morning to prep the engine and the VIP carriage, but hopefully we can get the pair of you aboard post-lunch. Is that okay?"

"Perfect," Miss Lacey said, allowing Jess's mom to drape the shawl across her rounded, old-lady shoulders and then escort her out into the hall.

As the door closed behind the pair, Jess stood in thought for a moment longer, then sagged back into her chair, a frown of uncertainty making a return appearance on her brow. The precise *reason* for that uncertainty continued to elude her though, still just a nebulous, niggling doubt, dancing somewhere at the edge of her awareness.

Maybe, in the end, it was simply a gut-level recognition of one of life's more sobering truths: that people who went around helping injured wildlife often ended up with a face full of claws...

4

Early Birds

"Oh, *bother,*" Vera Middleton muttered, taking an eraser to the accounts leger in front of her even as she cursed again her overactive hormones. Honestly though, half an hour ago it really hadn't seemed at all unreasonable—the notion of taking herself and her work outside into the spacious yard of Trans-Mars Haulage, where she could enjoy the pleasing warmth of a low morning sun while attempting to finalize last month's books.

Unfortunately, said notion had not taken into account the subsequent appearance of Sally Chu, intent on hosing down the Cannonball Express prior to today's charter job.

Sally Chu in micro-shorts and a tight-fitting t-shirt.

Now a tight-fitting *wet* t-shirt.

Nope. Complex mental arithmetic and a primed libido were *not* ideal bedfellows, Vera reflected…

… before going on to reflect at further dreamy length on the word *bedfellows*…

… then concluding the entire unhelpful routine in her habitual way with a thorough mental scolding: *Oh my goodness, girl, will you get a grip!*

Grabbing her pencil once more, Vera dragged her eyes away from the spectacle in question to focus again on the debit column of the leger. Because really (she told herself for what was surely the tenth time this morning), it wasn't as if someone as unfeasibly beautiful and self-assured as Sally 'The Rose of Tranquility' Chu—showgirl extraordinaire and object of desire for virtually anything with a pulse—could *ever* have the slightest romantic interest in someone as *un*-extraordinaire as Vera. Not even if she—

The hiss of Sally's hosepipe stopped suddenly, and a dead silence fell. A silence *not* charged in *any way* with *any kind* of entirely one-sided sexual tension whatsoever.

Nope. Absolutely not.

Forcing herself to stay focused on the pitifully limited charms of the leger's debit column, Vera detected a series of light footsteps as Sally stepped her way.

"What you reckon then, babe?" came the gal's throaty drawl.

"Oh, ehm, yes," Vera said as she looked up… her eyeballs going on to perform some truly Olympian gymnastics in their efforts to avoid the clinging wet t-shirt now less than one meter dead ahead. "Yes, looking good, Sally."

"Well, clearly," Sally said, "but what about the *train?*"

"What? I… No, I…" Vera's stomach turned over. "I didn't mean——"

"Vera, relax. It was a joke."

"Ha! … Yes, um, obviously I knew *that*. I was just—— *Jess!* There you are!"

Because yes! There (thank the gods of fortuitous interruption) she was—their trusty leader, rolling to a stop on the pushbike she'd just ridden into the TMH yard.

"Yeah, sorry I'm late," Jess said as she dismounted the cycle and straightened her disheveled overalls. "Took an age to finalize the route. But hey, all done now. So… I guess we better get that VIP car valeted before our passengers arrive, yes? Then we can— Huh? Something wrong?"

Her own puzzled frown having prompted the question, Vera glanced over at the glossy luxuriance of the Cannonball's VIP carriage, currently hitched between the sleeper wagon they used on long journeys and the ever-present crew car. "Um, it's a little late to be valeting the VIP car now, I'm afraid," Vera said. "Our passengers are already aboard."

Jess stared back in confusion. "What?"

"They were here when I arrived. I thought *you* must have let them in early."

Jess opened her mouth to reply, but before anything could emerge, one of the VIP carriage's polished mahogany doors swung open, and there was Miss Lacey.

"Ah, Ms. Flint, good morning," the old lady said. "I hope you don't mind. Sissy and I arrived rather early and found the gates open, so we thought we may as well settle ourselves in for the ride. That *was* all right, wasn't it?"

Vera saw the shadow of a frown pass over Jess's brow. But a moment later the big boss-lady of Trans-Mars Haulage just smiled and said, "Of course. Sure. No problem," then began to head over to the VIP car.

Vera followed, Sally too, and as the trio approached a smiling Miss Lacey in the carriage doorway, Vera suddenly found her gaze drawn by something else. Something *behind* one of the VIP car's curtained windows. Silhouetted against the closed floral drapes, reclining in the seat just beyond, was a lone figure in a coal scuttle bonnet.

Jess's eyes darted at once to the same silhouetted shape. "Is that your sister?" she asked Miss Lacey. "I'll maybe just say a quick hello and—"

But as Jess made to step up into the VIP car, Miss Lacey made no corresponding attempt to clear the doorway, instead lowering her voice to a near whisper and bending to speak into Jess's ear. Vera could just make out the words:

"In all honesty, Ms. Flint, I would really rather you didn't. Sissy dislikes being seen these days. In her youth she was regarded as something of a beauty, but since the smallpox outbreak of forty-three… Well… I'm sure you understand."

For a moment, Vera thought Jess might press the matter regardless, but then, as before, a business-like smile replaced Jess's puzzled frown, and she nodded. "Sure. Of course. Sorry."

"Thank you. You're very kind," Miss Lacey said and then closed the carriage door, leaving Jess… maybe not *concerned* exactly, Vera thought, but somehow not entirely happy either.

"Something wrong?" Vera asked.

It took another moment, but eventually Jess answered, "No… No, it's cool…" and turning to Vera and Sally, their ever-efficient leader pulled herself up straight, tucked her ponytail into her denim cap, and said, "Okay, team, let's get to it.

Leave at midday and we can be there sundown, no problemo. A nice, hassle-free charter. Easy money all the way. Just how we like it."

Ha! a rueful Vera would come to observe only a little later, once fate had dealt them what was surely the wildcard to end all wildcards. *Hassle-free indeed!*

For the next few hours though, hassle-free it was. With the entire train fully prepped by eleven, they all sat down to a sumptuous early lunch, care of Dave and his wondrous ways with a sandwich (not to mention his even *more* wondrous ways with coffee), and then at midday precisely, with a hiss of pistons and a clatter of wheels, the Cannonball Express, hauling a minimal train of only coal tender plus four wagons, pulled out of the TMH yard to steam its way north into the rocky wilds of the red planet.

Jess had scheduled herself and Sally to take the first shift together in the loco, which suited Vera fine. Being confined for two hours in the Cannonball's hot and sweaty cab with a hot and sweaty Sally Chu would, as far as Vera was concerned, be almost as much of a challenge to basic functioning as this morning's excruciating wet t-shirt fiasco.

Not that Vera would be putting her feet up for those first two hours though. A recent request from Dave had suggested a rather more active use of their mutual downtime, and now, while rugged Martian landscape rushed by outside the windows of the crew car, Vera stood there with said fellow in her arms as, once again, he did determined battle with both the basics of the foxtrot and Vera's gentle teasing.

"Look," the boy from Staines insisted between bouts of his trademark toe-mashing, "I just got *no idea* what you're talking about, Vera, okay?"

"Oh, come on, I'm not *blind,* you know," Vera replied as she steered him up the aisle of the crew car. "Left foot *slow...*" It was like steering a fully laden shopping trolley. With a wonky wheel. On a slope. In mud.

"Nope, not blind maybe," Dave came back, "just *highly* imaginative."

"You think I haven't noticed those little sighs you make around her?"

"I have a chest condition."

"And that twinkle in your eye?"

"Also an eye condition."

"Uh-huh," Vera said. "And so *this* particular venture—me teaching you how to dance—right foot *back,* please—is in no way whatsoever a Prince Charming gambit?"

"A *what?*"

"So you can sweep her off her feet at Tranquility's next 'royal ball'."

"Vera, get real. We both know *Jess's* Prince

Charming has got an Irish accent and a six-pack like the Hulk's personal trainer."

Well, yes, all right, Vera was not going to deny that, since encountering the unquestionably buff specimen of manhood on their very first outing in the Cannonball, Jess had indeed exhibited the significant hots for one Declan Donovan, leader of Mars's headline-grabbing underground activist group *Free Air,* and owner of the aforementioned accent and pack-of-six. Dave, however, did have at least one significant advantage over this admitted bookies' favorite, and while deftly dodging another potential foot-crunching, Vera reminded the lad of that advantage now. "Yes, but you're *here,*" she said, "and he *isn't.* You do know Jess hasn't seen Declan at all since that day. Not once. Apparently the chap hasn't even written. In *three months.*"

"Yeah, well… all completely irrelevant anyway, innit?" Dave replied. "Cos I say again, I do *not* have feelings for— JESS!" This last blurted out in wide-eyed shock, because, yes, of course, there she was, standing directly behind Vera, the very object of Dave's ill-concealed affections.

Vera felt Dave's chest begin to hitch, little stifled gasps punctuating the painfully few words that managed to fight their way out of his mouth:

"Jess <GASP> Hey! <GASP> we was just <GASP>…"

"You okay?" Jess asked him.

"He has a chest condition," Vera said, taking pity. "Also an eye condition. Personally, I'm not ruling out a lying-through-his-teeth condition, but there you go."

"Vera, can we talk?" Jess asked, that same not-quite-concerned-but-not-entirely-happy-either frown from before darkening her features once again.

"Of course," Vera said, allowing Jess to lead her away while Dave fought back another couple of wheezing gasps and tapped at his sternum for Jess's benefit: *Chest condition. See?*

As they settled into a seat at the far end of the crew car, Vera watched that peculiar look on Jess's face darken still further before finally asking her outright, "Jess, what is it? What's wrong?"

Leaning in and lowering her voice, Jess said, "Vera, I need you to do something for me…"

5

Sissy

Crouched in shadow at the far end of the VIP carriage's passageway, Jess watched in silence as Vera stepped up to the door of the car's luxury cabin. Pausing before the gleaming mahogany panel, Vera drew in a deep breath, raised a knuckle, then knocked gently.

And in response…

… not a sound. Just the ever-present clatter of wheels on track as the Cannonball Express steamed onward into the wilder northern regions of the red planet.

After a moment, Vera shot a nervous glance at Jess, who returned a curt nod of encouragement from her hiding place in the shadows. *Try again.*

Vera tried again, adding a tentative, "Um, excuse me, Miss Lacey?" into the bargain, and this time her efforts were rewarded with a rattle of keys from inside the cabin. A second later, the door creaked open a fraction, and Jess saw Vera fire up one of her winning smiles.

"I'm so sorry to bother you, Miss Lacey," Vera said, "but it seems I need your signature on an addendum to the contract."

Miss Lacey's soft, old-lady voice came back in reply, somewhat hesitant: "Oh... well, yes, of course. Do you... do you have it there?"

"Ah. Sorry, no," Vera said. "It's just on my desk though. Do you mind? It really won't take a minute," and dialing her winning smile up a notch, Vera gestured towards the far end of the passageway—the end where Jess wasn't.

A further moment of silence followed, during which Miss Lacey, not visible from Jess's vantage point, seemed to consider Vera's request. But eventually, "Of course. If it'll just take a minute," the old lady said and stepped out of the compartment into the corridor. "Back in a second, Sissy," she called over her shoulder, before pulling the cabin door closed behind her and locking it with the passenger key Jess had given her that morning. This done, Miss Lacey pocketed the same key then smiled up at Vera, who nodded her thanks and began to lead the old lady off down the corridor.

"Just this way," Vera said, that smile of hers never wavering as she opened the door at the corridor's far end to usher Miss Lacey through.

Jess watched the pair of them disappear into the crew car, saw the door click shut behind them, then waited a full ten seconds more before finally stepping out from her hiding place.

Chewing on her lower lip in a kind of low-level, nonspecific apprehension—she genuinely had *no idea* what to expect here—Jess crept up to the locked door of the VIP cabin, placed both palms and one ear against its wooden surface, and listened...

Nothing.

At least, nothing she could hear above the rumbling rattle of the Cannonball.

With her heartrate shifting on up into second gear—again for reasons that remained entirely obscure—Jess took in a deep breath, knocked lightly, and called, "Hello?"—

—upon which there came from behind the door a low rush of sounds—several heavy thuds, a rustle, a creak or two, and then...

... silence once more.

After another moment, Jess knocked again. "Hello?"

But this time, nothing.

31

The silence stretched on…

Okay then, Jess thought, *you leave me no choice here, folks,* and glancing about her to check she was still alone, she withdrew her master set of keys from a pocket, unlocked the cabin door, and pushed it open just a crack.

"Um, hey, really sorry to bother you like this, but my name is Jess. I'm the train's chief engineer, yes? Kind of the boss, if you like. So I'm coming in, okay?" and shoving the door open a little farther, Jess eased herself into the cabin.

As had been the case since Jess's arrival at TMH that morning, all of the VIP carriage's curtains were fully closed, shadow and gloom blanketing the compartment in a sinister monochrome.

"I… I guess I just wanna say hello," Jess continued, "if that's okay with you. And maybe—" She stopped, her confusion growing, her heartrate lurching its way up into third. Because with her eyes now growing accustomed to the low light, Jess should surely have been able to make out the presence of the carriage's other occupant. The mysterious Sissy.

But she couldn't. There was no one there.

The entire cabin appeared completely empty.

Jess felt a tinge of irritation. "Okay, look, I did *hear* you, you know. I just want to—"

And that was when she saw it.

A figure.

Dark and silent.

Clad in a long plain dress and a coal scuttle bonnet—

—and clinging to the ceiling directly above her.

Cursing in shock, Jess threw herself backwards just as the figure dropped from the ceiling, feet first, to hit the floor with a room-shaking thud. Then, before Jess had time even to cry out, a monstrous animal shriek tore at the air as the creature—all fangs and fur and razor claws; part gorilla, part wolfman—rose up to its full height and hurled itself forward.

With a scream of terror, Jess darted to one side, the monster flying past and slamming into the cabin wall, where it slumped to the floor in a rain of shattered woodwork. Shaking its bonneted head, the thing yowled in fury, and as it began again to rise, Jess whirled where she stood, making a desperate dive for the still open carriage door. But even as her front foot was crossing the threshold, she felt something—one of the creature's claws, it could be nothing else—hook the rear shoulder straps of her denim overalls. The move brought Jess up short with brutal efficiency, forcing all the air from her lungs in a loud, barking gasp. Then, with a single mighty tug, Jess was yanked off her feet and went flying backwards, sailing across the width of the cabin to crash headfirst into one of its curtained windows.

Jess both heard and felt the muffled crunch as the glass behind the curtain gave way, and an instant later, in a tangle of floral drapes and curtain cords, she was tumbling through the window, out into the wild rush of air blasting its way down the side of the speeding train. Twisting mid-fall, Jess flung out a desperate hand and somehow managed to grab the sill of the cabin's shattered window, her body slamming down onto the carriage exterior, the rocky surface of Mars rushing by just meters below.

Grimacing in pain, winded almost to incapacitation, and with blood seeping from arms lacerated by the shattered window glass, Jess clung on, her booted feet scrabbling for some kind of purchase—*any* kind of purchase—on the carriage's external paneling. But there was none. Nothing but smooth, shiny mahogany. And beneath that, nothing but certain death on the red planet's boulder-strewn ground, hurtling past at close to one hundred kilometers per hour. Shifting her grip on the window sill, Jess fought for a better hold, finally found one, and, with every muscle straining, dragged herself up level with the broken window.

But even as her head rose above the sill, there again was the creature, filling the window frame, fangs bared, claws unsheathed, eyes ablaze with a blind animal fury. Letting loose another ear-shattering roar, the creature fixed its ferocious gaze on Jess dangling from the window sill and locked both of its claws together into a single titanic fist—a fist that could surely pummel granite to a pulp, never mind flesh and bone. Then, its bulging muscles taut with power, the creature roared for a third time, raised high that pile-driver of a double-fist, and brought it pounding down at Jess's head.

6

Runaways

"SISSY, NO!"

The cry rang out from behind the enraged creature, and like a prisoner caught in a watchtower spotlight, the animal froze where it stood, its fearsome double-fist coming to a halt halfway down its path to Jess's skull.

In the cabin doorway stood the tiny figure of Miss Lacey, her elderly body rigid with tension, her features scrunched into a look of severest disapproval. But while the old lady's cry had clearly given the thing pause, still the monster in the dress and the coal scuttle bonnet stood there, growling its feral fury as it glared down at Jess dangling from the shattered window.

Once again Miss Lacey raised her voice, "I said NO, Sissy! Stop this right now!" and once again the woman's admonishing tone seemed to arrest the creature, which, though still growling, shot a glance over its shoulder, eyeing the old lady in the doorway—

—who, in her turn, followed through on the verbal warning with a single arched eyebrow—the kind you might direct at a stubborn child who refused to do their chores.

Something seemed to flicker across the creature's face then. *Doubt, maybe?* Jess thought. *Regret, even?*

"Sissy, that is *quite enough,*" Miss Lacey said, an air of weary exasperation replacing the anger and disapproval of her previous words. "Come here, girl. Come to mommy," upon which, with a final sigh-like grunt, all the rage seemed to leave the monster at once, its arms drooping to its sides, its shoulders sagging, and what Jess could have sworn was a look of shame creeping into its dark eyes.

Retreating from the smashed window, the creature vocalized again—this time a kind of low, heartfelt mewl—before turning to Miss Lacey in the cabin doorway, loping over to her, then finally stepping into the old woman's open arms.

With the window now clear, Jess dragged herself the rest of the way through into the wrecked compartment, where she slumped gasping onto the glass and splinter strewn floor—

—while opposite her in the open doorway, Miss Lacey held the trembling monster to her breast and stroked the creature's silver-gray fur:

"There there, Sissy. It's over now. It's all over…"

•••

"I realize now I should have been honest with you all from the start," Miss Lacey said, "and for that I am truly sorry. But please, I beg you, do not forsake Sissy because of *my* foolish misjudgment."

It was close to half an hour later, the train now tucked away in the first convenient siding they'd come to following the 'incident', and with a silent Sissy nestled in by her feet, the old lady—though not nearly so old as her earlier 'helpless granny' affectations had contrived to make out—sat huddled in a corner of the crew car, telling her strange tale to Jess and the gang, while an appropriately gothic thunderstorm raged outside, and rain lashed at the carriage windows.

Quite the tragic tale of horror it was too, Jess would be forced to concede, and despite the woman's previous deceit, not to mention its near fatal consequences, Jess couldn't help but feel her heart go out to the unlikely pair before them. That this was the full unvarnished truth they were finally hearing from their troubled client, Jess had little doubt. The sheer rawness of the pain on display in the old lady's eyes was evidence aplenty in that regard.

As for Sissy herself, since nearly sending Jess to a brutal and bloody demise on the rocky surface of Mars, the creature had been quite the picture of loving serenity, her face—somehow both beautiful and fearsome at the same time— suggesting in repose an emotional intelligence that, through the subtlety and complexity of its expression, seemed almost *human* to Jess. Not that this made the animal's continued presence among them any less intimidating. Maybe one meter seventy when she stood upright, her slender frame rippling with dense musculature beneath silver-gray fur, Sissy's resemblance to a horror movie wolfman (or wolf*woman* in this case) remained both remarkable and unnerving, the creature's gingham dress and floral bonnet doing little to undermine the aura of monstrous strength and animal pride she radiated, even in her currently tranquil state.

Dave refilled Miss Lacey's coffee cup from the steaming jug in his hands, and after sipping gratefully at the aromatic brew, the not-quite-so-old-after-all woman resumed:

"I mean it, Ms. Flint. I really do. If Sissy were forced to go back there, I honestly don't think she would…" Her voice trailed off into silence, while at her feet, Sissy let out a low mournful cry, nuzzling deeper into the old woman's side.

"Something happened, didn't it?" Jess said. "At this carnival of yours."

"Yes. Yes, it did. No one died, thank goodness, but Sissy… The problem is, she's now fast approaching full sexual maturity, her hormones are raging, and in all honesty, it's only a matter of time before someone does. *Die,* I mean. And after that…" Something almost fully physical seemed to leave Miss Lacey's huddled body then, and she slumped back into her seat, tears—*real* tears this time—brimming in her eyes. "They won't even use a needle, Ms. Flint. Just a shotgun and a heavy duty refuse sack."

Swallowing hard, Jess found herself at an utter loss, and a bleak, lengthy silence fell, relieved only by the drumming of rain on the carriage roof. At last, Jess rose, paced the floor for several seconds more, then turned and delivered what was really the only response she could possibly give in the circumstances: "Miss Lacey, I'm so sorry, but to continue here would put my entire crew in jeopardy. Not to mention my haulage license, her—*Sissy*—being stolen property an' all."

"Please," Miss Lacey implored. "Ms. Flint, I *beg* you. I have no one else to turn to. You really are my only hope. *Sissy's* only hope…"

And once again, a dark silence descended, every set of eyes in the carriage boring into Jess, awaiting the boss's *final* final answer. Heaving out a massive sigh, Jess chewed on her lower lip for another long moment, then turned to the crew car's side door—the one that led outside. Rain or no rain, Jess needed some air, and stepping forward, she pushed the door open…

… only to recoil with a start of shock as the barrel of a gleaming six-shooter rose to meet her widening-eyes.

"Well howdy there, young lady," Levi Zabulon Slinger said as he cocked the gun's hammer.

7

Zora

Slinger, a study in immaculately tailored black, stood there blocking the doorway of the crew car, rain ricocheting off the brim of his waxed Stetson as a smile played across his thin lips.

"What the hell," Jess gasped, her heart pounding. "What are you—"

"Keep your hands where I can see 'em, girlie," the private-hire enforcer said, his easy drawl at chilling odds with the menace in his eyes. "So I'm guessing you know the drill, right? No sudden moves, and step *slowly* back into the carriage." As the man spoke, the revolver he held leveled at Jess's head stayed almost supernaturally steady, while his remaining arms—the scumbag had a freakish six in total, care of some deeply illegal body-augmentation surgery—hovered over his other five pistols, still at rest in the mother-of-pearl encrusted holsters strapped in two lines of three down the gunman's pant legs.

Seeing no immediate alternative—at least, none that wouldn't involve blood, screaming, and almost certain death—Jess followed Slinger's orders and stepped back. At the same time, in the carriage behind her, Sally, Vera, and Dave scrambled to their feet in stunned silence, while over in the corner, Sissy mewled in fear, cowering into Miss Lacey.

"What is this?" Jess growled. "What the hell do you want here, Slinger?"

"Why, what I always want, girlie. Plain old-fashioned customer satisfaction," upon which the man's eyes shifted to take in Sissy, still huddled in terror by Miss Lacey's feet. The sight of the whimpering creature seemed to please the gunman, and smiling wider still, Slinger turned to call over his shoulder, "Well, all rightie, and that would be a big ol' happy affirmative. Critter's right here, babe. In you come."

And in she came.

Even through the spiraling confusion of the moment itself, Jess couldn't help but reflect that if Slinger knew how to make a dramatic entrance—

and regrettably, Jess had seen enough of those to know for certain that he did—his skills were as nothing compared to the individual who joined them now in the carriage. Unnervingly tall, ramrod straight of back, and radiating a sense of entitlement that made Jess feel about five years old, the woman swept into the crew car like the President of Everywhere. Exuding disdain and impatience in equal measure, Slinger's associate arrived stage center in just three commanding strides, her long leather coat falling into stillness around her spurred bootheels as she studied the group arrayed before her. Studied them with starkest disapproval.

"Ms. Flint," Slinger said, "may I introduce—"

"No, you may not, Zab," the newcomer snapped. "What is this? The ambassador's frickin reception?" and turning to address Jess, the woman continued in similar vein, focused as a laser, arresting as a shotgun blast: "Zora Petrovna, legal owner of the stolen property that you appear to be transporting here, young woman." A brief sally over her shoulder at Slinger came next: "Also, Zab, 'babe' me again, you lose body parts. The good ones."

Jess frowned. "Um, okay, look—"

"Just trying to be friendly, Zora," Slinger drawled.

"Yeah?" the woman came back. "Try being not-a-sleazeball-jerk, Zab. Just this once, okay?" after which, following a brief eyes-closed moment to compose herself, Slinger's compatriot aimed her weaponized vocals at a fresh target, this time the pair of cowering figures in the carriage's corner seat. "Annie. Sissy. So, as they say, we can do this the hard way, or—"

But before the woman could finish, the creature in the corner leapt to her clawed feet and, with a roar of animal fury, launched herself forward.

"SISSY, NO!" Miss Lacey yelled, but the old lady's cry came too late, and what happened next was something that would remain branded in Jess's memory for the rest of her life—a moment of such shocking and sudden violence it left her shaken to her core.

From a kind of holster arrangement on her belt, the woman called Zora Petrovna whipped out a long dark object tipped with metal spikes, jabbing it forward at the creature who barreled towards her. As the object's mace-like end pierced the material of Sissy's dress, there was a loud SNAP, a crackle of electricity, and with an anguished howl, the monster not only broke off her attack but threw herself shrieking back into the corner, shredded cotton and silver-gray fur smoking where the electric cattle prod had made contact.

For several long seconds, no one spoke, the

grim silence an unwelcome opportunity for Jess to ponder one of Mars's crueler ironies—that while its EMP-riddled atmosphere negated the use of even the simplest electronics, high-voltage static discharges, be they from lightning bolts or illegal cattle prods, were unaffected.

Eventually, Slinger took a step forward. "Well okay, so let's get to it then, shall we?" and reaching into a shoulder bag, he produced several sets of handcuffs, throwing them all in a pile at the feet of Jess and her crew. "Wrists *and* ankles, people," Slinger said, drawing three more of his revolvers to level one each at Sally, Vera, and Dave.

Still seeing no way out of the situation, Jess nodded to the others, who began in sullen silence to reach for the handcuffs on the floor.

"And Zora," Slinger said, not without a touch of rancor, "tranq the dang yeti, would ya?"

Raising a warning eyebrow at her lawman-for-hire—clearly this was a woman who did not *take* orders—Zora nonetheless drew a small plastic case from her coat pocket, and as she flipped it open, Jess caught a glimpse of its foam-padded contents: three fresh syringes and a small glass drug bottle.

Still brandishing the cattle prod in her other hand, Zora turned once more to Sissy, favoring the creature with the iciest of smiles. "Okay, girl. Now this won't hurt a—"

But again, Sissy reared up howling and threw herself headlong at Zora, who countered as before, lunging with the cattle prod. This time though, the woman wasn't content to issue just a single warning strike. Stepping forward to follow her screaming victim back into the corner of the crew car, Zora stabbed out again and again with the device, Sissy's howls of agony rending the air as she convulsed and thrashed with the repeat shocks.

"No! Please! No more!" Miss Lacey screamed, her desperate efforts to shield Sissy thwarted as Slinger grabbed the old woman by the hair, throwing her to the floor.

And still Zora kept thrusting the crackling, snapping device at the defenseless animal, Sissy shrieking and flailing and—

"ENOUGH! STOP!"

But this time it wasn't Miss Lacey's voice.

It wasn't Jess's either.

It was Dave's.

Eyes ablaze with a fury Jess could barely believe he had in him, the fella from Staines took a lurching step towards the woman torturing Sissy.

But a single step was as far as he got, because even as he was raising his back foot to take another, the barrel of one of Slinger's revolvers shoved itself into the soft flesh of Dave's left cheek, and Sissy's would-be savior froze.

8

The Right Thing

Withdrawing the cattle prod from the creature at her feet, Zora Petrovna turned to the fear-frozen figure of Dave, assessing the guy with a single contemptuous once up and down as the traumatized Sissy sank whimpering into Miss Lacey's arms.

"*Really,* young fella?" Zora said. "And what, pray tell, is your function around here?"

Jess watched Dave blink several times in mute terror, his lungs snatching at the air in ragged gasps while the muzzle of Slinger's six-shooter compressed the pale flesh of his jowl. Two drops of sweat trailed down from Dave's sodden hairline to break on the gun's gleaming barrel.

But then, taking everyone by surprise—himself among them, Jess suspected—Dave somehow managed to straighten, and gulping back the worst of his fear, he looked Zora dead in the eye:

"Me? I'm Dave," he said. "I make the coffee," of which, Jess saw, there was still a large steaming jug in his clenched right fist.

A large steaming jug which he proceeded to tip all over Zora's cattle prod hand.

With a shriek of pain, Zora leapt backwards, dropping the prod and colliding hard with Slinger, whose single retaliating gunshot, ear-shattering in the enclosed carriage, went wild, punching a hole in the metal ceiling.

Then, before anyone else could move, Dave dropped to the floor, grabbed the fallen cattle prod, and jammed it hard into Slinger's chest.

To say that what followed caught them all off guard would, Jess later reflected, be something of an understatement. Possibly, Dave had expected Slinger just to slump unconscious to the floor after a single shock from the prod. Or go flying across the carriage to knock himself out on a wall panel.

But neither of those things was what happened. And among the crew of the Cannonball Express, what *did* happen went down in company legend.

Hollering in pain, and with the sparking cattle prod pressed to his chest, the multi-armed gunslinger began to convulse on the spot, every one of his occupied trigger fingers clenching and re-clenching with ongoing involuntary spasms. Hot flying lead pounded the carriage in all directions, tearing through panelwork, shattering windows, denting steel and brass. As broken glass and splintered wood rained down, the car's other occupants—Zora included—dived for whatever cover they could find, keeping their heads low until, almost ten full seconds later, with every last one of Slinger's chambered rounds spent, the gunsmoke-filled carriage resembled nothing less than a swiss cheese on wheels. There followed, briefly, a further series of impotent clicks from the now emptied weapons, after which, still convulsing, and with a string of drool dangling from one corner of his slack mouth, Slinger finally slumped to the floor of the car and lay still.

But the entire ordeal wasn't quite over yet, because just as the gunman's head thudded into the floorboards, Zora leapt from her cover to make a desperate lunge for Dave.

"Look out!" Jess yelled, and even as the words were leaving her lips, Dave whirled on the wild-eyed figure surging towards him, thrusting the cattle prod into her stomach. Electricity crackled, fizzed, snapped, while at the same time Zora gave out a protracted shriek of agony, finally sagging to the floor atop the unmoving Slinger. And there, for the moment, the charming pair lay, breathing at least, Jess could see, but otherwise out for the proverbial count.

A stunned silence fell, all remaining eyes in the bullet-riddled crew car now fixed upon Dave, who, for his part, stood there agog at the center of the carnage, shaking and gasping, cattle prod still smoking in his hands.

Sally was the one who finally found words, though, as ever with Sal, not perhaps the most helpful ones in the circumstances: "Holy freakin crap, Dave, what the hell did you *do?*"

And still the guy just stood there, staring back at them all as if he genuinely had *no idea* what he'd done.

After another moment, Jess pulled herself to her feet, stepped up to the shell-shocked Dave, and extracted the cattle prod from his trembling clutches. This done, she turned again to the others and offered them a dark-toned but earnest answer to Sally's hanging question:

"The right thing," Jess said. "*That's* what he did. The right thing."

And did anyone disagree? No, they did not. How could they?

Five minutes later, a pair of limp bodies—one with six arms, one the regulation two—went sailing from the door of the crew car to land with a thud in the dirt by the rails.

Jess and Sally followed, leaping down to the graveled trackside, where rain still pounded and thunder still rumbled, and where, just a little way off, there stood an empty jail wagon behind two visibly skittish horses. Slinger and Zora had clearly come prepared, Jess thought, and must have driven in unheard over the sound of the storm.

Unhitching the two animals from the wagon, Jess and Sal slapped the beasts' rumps, and with a toss of their water-logged manes, both horses galloped off, vanishing into the rain-drenched haze.

"Okay, let's get the hell outta here," Jess said, and hightailing it for the loco with Sally, the pair hauled themselves up into the cab, where Jess's hands began to fly over the Cannonball's controls.

"Please tell me you got a plan here," Sally said as she reached for her coal shovel.

Jess just laughed and shot her friend a wry look. "Seriously? Evil circus owners? Monsters in frocks? Dave goes Ninja? Sal, I swear god himself is making this up as he goes," and working the engine's controls a little more, Jess was rewarded with a deafening blast of steam and a clank of pistons as the Cannonball Express came to heart-stirring life around her, lurching forward into the gathering storm.

9

Maybe Just a Bit of Gapping

"And that's her when she was two," Miss Lacey said, "long before that awful Hellbeast of Mars routine the management dreamed up once she'd lost her baby looks. Oh, but the audiences adored her back then. It's not hard to see why, of course."

Slurping down the last of her coffee, Sally Chu studied the picture before her—just one of hundreds in a bulging photo album that Miss Lacey, with endearing maternal pride, had insisted Sally and Dave look through. In the photo, a young Sissy, maybe as tall as a human two-year-old, stood on perfect point, posing in a pink ballet tutu, while in the background, a tent full of delighted onlookers took to their feet, applauding. And yes, Sally could only agree, it wasn't at all hard to see why audiences had fallen in love with the critter. Li'l thing was cuter than a basket full of guinea pigs. With bows in their hair. Speaking Japanese.

Leaning back so Dave could get a closer look at the album, Sally took the moment to smile across at Sissy herself—once more crouched at Miss Lacey's feet—before glancing up at the speeding crew car's sole surviving window, in whose brass frame the cratered landscape of northern Mars continued to flash by, a deep red in the low sun. Six hours on from dumping Slinger and Zora trackside, during which time they'd all done what they could to patch up the bullet-riddled crew car, the Martian evening was well and truly settling in, and by Sally's reckoning, it couldn't be too long now before they actually arrived at their destination.

"I did so love that act," Miss Lacey continued, her eyes lowered, her knotted old-lady hands working away at a long piece of knitting that dangled from two fat needles. Some kind of chunky scarf, Sally guessed; it was difficult to tell. "She always was a beautiful mover," Miss Lacey went on. "Graceful like you wouldn't believe. Like…" but her voice trailed off, and she drew in a long shaky breath, setting her knitting aside on a table by her elbow.

"Something wrong?" Sally asked.

Miss Lacey turned to Sally but then looked down again. "It's just… it was all so *wrong,* wasn't it? So… *unnatural.*"

Glancing over at Dave, Sally exchanged a look of puzzlement with the guy, before the pair of them turned their mutual gaze on Sissy, nestled in by Miss Lacey's legs and pretty as a picture in her gingham dress and floral bonnet. Dave spoke for both himself and Sally when he asked, "So, um… no offence but… how come you're still dressing her like *that* then?"

A bark of ironic but not unkind laughter broke Miss Lacey's pensive mood. "Ha! You really think *I* get a say in what she wears? She's a teenager now. She grew up around human women. These days she will express her femininity any way she damn well pleases."

Sally smiled. "I am liking this gal more and more. It's almost as if—" but the clatter of an opening door interrupted, and Sally turned with the others to see Vera step into the crew car.

Resplendent in her oil-smudged denims, the British gal came tramping through from the train's loco end sporting a weary but satisfied smile, and almost instantly, Sally felt a familiar tension steal its way into her body—the same tension she'd felt from the very first day she'd met Vera Middleton. Because, honest to god, it truly was like the gal had some kind of secret, behind-the-scenes styling team working on her every frickin entrance: the lone dab of soot on her alabaster cheek could quite easily have been placed there by a movie makeup artist as the final killer blow of irresistible cute; and let's not even get *started* on her exquisitely disarranged hair, tumbling from a single straining scrunchie like— *Dammit, Sal, just get a frickin grip, girl, would ya?* It wasn't even as if the reserved and soft-spoken English lesbian had ever shown the *slightest* interest in Sally. Quite the opposite, in fact. After almost three months working together, Sally had still spent barely any significant time alone with Vera during which the gal hadn't frozen up in apparent distaste and struggled to make even the lightest of conversation. All of which led to one inevitable and depressing conclusion: that Trans-Mars Haulage's resident posh gal, while painfully polite in everyday exchanges, regarded Sally simply as beneath her—just some trailer-trash slut-bunny, barely worth talking to.

Yeah, well *screw her*…

Stifling a sigh, and in the interests of keeping things relaxed, Sally offered a simple, "Hey, girl. That time already?" to which the vision in coal dust and perspiration replied:

"'Fraid so, Sally. Thy shovel awaits."

Okay, good enough, Sally thought. *No visible recoiling at least,* and rising to her feet, she grabbed her work overalls and began to wriggle her way into them.

A moment later, Dave rose too, an excited smile breaking out across his boyish features as he stepped up to Vera. "Hey, guess what, V? Think I finally got the hang of it. That *natural turn* thing in the foxtrot, yeah? Look…" and as Vera began to haul off her workboots, Dave set about demonstrating the dance move in the aisle of the carriage, miming an invisible partner while Vera looked on with ever patient interest.

"See? Better, right?" Dave said once he'd worked the whole step through.

"Mmmm, well done, very close, but you're not *quite* there yet," Vera answered, dumping her boots in a corner and rising. "What you have to remember is—"

But she got no further. Because just as the gal took Dave into hold, Sissy, still crouched at Miss Lacey's feet, let out a sudden and unexpected growl of anger, surging up onto her hairy haunches and springing towards the startled pair.

"Whoah!" Vera cried out, backing away quickly from both Dave and Sissy—

—in response to which Sissy appeared to regain her calm, dropping back and settling down once more at Miss Lacey's feet, from where she continued to glower at Vera.

Vera shot Miss Lacey a look of concern. "Um…

what was *that?*"

Placing a soothing hand on Sissy's shoulder, Miss Lacey offered Vera an apologetic sigh. "I am *so* sorry," she said. "Truth be told, I *was* a little worried that this might happen."

"That *what* might happen?" a mystified Vera asked.

"I'm rather afraid Sissy may now regard *you* as a sexual rival."

At which Vera—not surprisingly, Sally would allow—positively goggled. "*Excuse* me?"

"For Dave," Miss Lacey said.

"Well, *obviously* for Dave."

"*Obviously?*" Sally put in, unable to stop herself. "*Really?*"

"Oi! Standing right here," the guy himself complained.

Clearing her throat, Miss Lacey sought to explain further: "After all, the young man *did* present a somewhat conspicuous display of his masculinity earlier."

"He *did?*" Sally said. "That guy and his winky…"

Miss Lacey favored Sally with a look of deepest disapproval before proceeding: "By *protecting* Sissy. Protecting the whole tribe, in fact."

"Oh boy, this is too good," Sally said, shaking her head in amusement then glancing over at Dave, who by now was swelling visibly with some considerable pride. "Dave, my man, you have *pulled!*" and reaching forward, Sally pinched the guy's chubby cheek, prompting a further threatening growl from Sissy. "Steady there, sister," Sally growled back at the creature. "He is *all yours.* Just, you know, be *gentle* with him, okay?"

"Yeah, yeah, very funny," a scowling Dave muttered as Sally, unable to rein in her widening grin, retreated a step and began to pull on her workboots, all the while drinking in the entirely unexpected and *highly* entertaining scene still playing out before her:

"Um, is she going to be all right here?" Vera asked Miss Lacey, firing a nervous glance at Sissy.

"You two just carry on," Miss Lacey replied with a reassuring smile. "I'll handle Sissy."

Clearly *not* reassured in any way, shape, or form, Vera nonetheless nodded, stepped forward into Dave's arms—

—and another dark growl emerged from the monster in the coal scuttle bonnet.

"Sissy..." Miss Lacey warned, the creature quietening again, albeit with a distinct air of sulky teenage reluctance.

Eventually, Vera managed a somewhat nervous tremolo: "Okay then, Dave, so from the top, yes? Two-three-four, right foot forward, left foot to the side..." and off they went down the aisle.

Grinning wider still as she took all of this in,

Sally double-knotted her right bootlace, rose to her feet, and finally headed away up the carriage for her shift in the loco with Jess, the last exchange her wagging ears remained a party to running roughly as follows:

Vera: "Good, Dave, that's very good…"

Dave: "This is weird…"

Vera: "Watch your frame now. No gapping."

Sissy: "GRRRRRRRRRRRRRRRR."

Vera: "Okay, so maybe just a *bit* of gapping…"

10

The Town With No Name

Not, he would admit, in one of his sunnier moods, Levi Zabulon Slinger ripped another timber slat from the rail siding's perimeter fence, added it to those already tucked under his other arms, then turned and trudged his way back to the dwindling signal fire he'd built god knew how many hours ago when the dark of the Martian night had begun to close in.

Reclining by said fire, and puffing away at a cigar the size of a baby's arm (right now, Slinger wasn't convinced the woman wouldn't smoke an *actual* baby's arm, should the opportunity ever present itself), Zora Petrovna barely acknowledged Slinger's presence as he approached. And even when he dropped the timber (irritably, he would be forced to concede) onto the flickering flames, still the woman just lounged there in the firelight's glow, gazing up at the night sky like the Queen of the Holy Universe and looking for all the world as if she were somehow mentally conducting the distant thunder and lightning that continued to rumble behind the clouds.

Dang and blast the woman, Slinger thought, wiping his sweaty brow and glowering down at her recumbent form. "Really, Zora? Think you could maybe lend a hand here?"

Puffing out a billowing cloud large enough to mount a significant armed assault under, Zora allowed a moment for the cigar smoke to clear then smiled back at Slinger. "Gee, dunno, Zab. Think you could maybe not screw around with the fangirls and ruin a perfectly good showbiz marriage? Oh, wait…"

Great, Slinger thought, groaning inwardly. *Just great.* And was it even the *first* time Zora had raised this particular subject in the nosediving course of today's events? Was it heck! It certainly wouldn't be the last either, that was for dang sure. With a further weary sigh, Slinger took a moment to adjust the emergency breather unit fitted beneath his nose (the air quality around the siding had dipped dramatically in the past hour), after which, slumping down next to Zora, he finally asked the obvious: "You do know there's plenty other private-hire lawmen you coulda signed up for this job, right?"

"What, and miss our sparkling repartee?" the woman answered. And by 'repartee', of course, she meant laser-targeted ball-busting. "Where's the fun in that?" And by 'fun' she meant gleefully sadistic satisfaction. Wasn't even as if Slinger could have said no to her. Dang woman had ways of making a fella's life a misery, long range or point blank.

"You know what *your* problem is, Zab?" Zora continued, and once again, Slinger gave an inward groan, painfully aware that his ex-wife maintained a substantial and ever-growing mental list of these so-called 'problems' and that she was highly unlikely to stop at pointing out just the one.

As fortune would have it, however, before Zora could begin the character assassination proper, a sound from above—a kind of droning whine—caught the attention of them both, and when they looked up, an airplane dipped into view beneath the low clouds. Even in the near monochrome of the gathering darkness, the craft's markings were unmistakable—it was the Petrovna's Carnival biplane—and as Slinger watched, the airplane zoomed directly over where he and Zora lay by the signal fire, gave a prominent wing wiggle to indicate that the pilot had spotted them, then flew off again into the evening gloom.

"Well, okay," Slinger said. "So the cavalry's on its way, the larger problem being, of course, that we still don't know exactly where our Ms. Flint is headed now." And they didn't. Until recently, Zora's two runaways had left a trail warm enough for anyone with even the slightest investigative gumption to follow—a string of reliable witnesses had readily recognized the old woman in the headshots that Zora had supplied, leading Slinger quickly to Tranquility, where further enquiries had revealed the woman's hiring of Trans-Mars Haulage. Now however, with the chartered train having overshot its final scheduled stop and heading out, *un*scheduled, into the northern Free Zones, the runaways' *new* destination remained a mystery.

Well, to *Slinger,* at least. Not, apparently, to Zora though, who, expelling another prodigious lungsworth of cigar smoke, spat into the fire then threw Slinger the kind of look that would have withered men with fewer arms and less ordnance:

"Oh, come on, Zab, what the hell am I even paying you for? This far north? Only one possible place it *could* be…"

•••

"The Town With No Name? That's what they actually *call* it?"

Jess's incredulous tone was mirrored times three in the frowning faces of the rest of the gang, who, along with Miss Lacey and Sissy, stood peering at the spectacle before them while the Cannonball Express sat cooling at their backs.

The spectacle in question consisted of a small, currently empty town square—rutted, muddy, and strewn with litter and filth—around which were clustered various ramshackle buildings. Most of these buildings appeared to be little more than hastily constructed timber shacks, and even in the gloom of the Martian night, Jess could see that the majority of them were riddled with rot and bullet holes, nary a surviving piece of intact window glass evident on even one of their peeling facades. Adding to this air of moldering decrepitude, a variety of badly painted signs clung haphazardly to several of these decaying structures, like maimed and mutilated casualties of battle about to slump to their deaths in the mud below:

HOT GUNS - INTIRELY UNTRACEABLE

DRUGS'R'US

THE CREETURE GUY - DICE'N'SPLICE YOOR OWN!

Shaking her head in distaste, Jess said again, "The Town With No Name? *Seriously?*"

Miss Lacey nodded, wrapping a protective arm around Sissy beside her. "This ugly little settlement has never officially existed, Ms. Flint. Ever. And those who trade here pay handsomely to keep it off all maps, official *and* unofficial. What else should they have called it?"

Sally grimaced at the mud and filth at their feet. "Jeez, I dunno, how about The Town With No Sanitation. The Town With No Self-Respect. The Town With No Frickin' Spell-Checker. Lady, this place stinks in every possible way."

"Oh, yes, no question," Miss Lacey said, "but if you are in the market for something illegal— *anything* illegal—well then... welcome to Macy's."

Jess glanced at her wristband air monitor, which was currently showing a steady yellow. "Atmosphere's breathable at least. Guess they got a generator here somewhere."

Miss Lacey nodded. "Total independence. They rely on no one but themselves. On which subject: I say again, Ms. Flint, I am more than happy to take care of things myself from here. You really could have just dropped us at New Dakota as scheduled."

But Jess was having none of that. Not after the horror of the cattle prod incident. Even now, nearly seven hours later, Jess still felt a lingering sense of shame that she hadn't stepped up immediately when Miss Lacey had revealed the truth of Sissy's plight. "Nuh-uh," Jess said. "You wanna take Sissy home, we *take* Sissy home. So… what now?"

By way of an answer, Miss Lacey grasped Sissy's hand then took a step forward, leading the group out of the rail siding the Cannonball Express stood parked in and off across the filth-sodden square of The Town With No Name.

Just a few squelching paces in, as they neared the square's center, several looming, boxy shapes began to emerge from the gloom there, and two steps later, Jess found herself contemplating a collection of battered metal cages in varying shapes and sizes, all of them set out in a line, as if on display. Some of these cages lay empty, while others contained… well, truth be told, Jess wasn't entirely sure *what* the occupied cages contained. Creatures like nothing she'd ever seen before. Like nothing she'd ever *imagined* before. Hairy, scaly, feathered, fanged, the works. A full-on medieval bestiary, of both blood-chilling horror and bewildering beauty. As Jess and the group shuffled past them, most of the captive creatures—from giant eyeless leech-like monstrosities to beguiling four-winged bird/butterfly hybrids—simply lay there as if doped into submission, only a few of the caged specimens displaying any visible signs of defiance, either moaning in distress or hurling themselves listlessly at the bars of their prisons. Jess noted also that many of these 'prisons' sported FOR SALE signs, messily executed in a bright, glow-in-the-dark emulsion, several unopened cans of which sat beside a few of the more freshly painted efforts.

"This place, I am now utterly ashamed to say, is where we originally bought Sissy," Miss Lacey explained. "The whole town here sprang up around the creature trade, and rumor has it the principal source of all these poor animals is somewhere close by."

Pausing by the last cage in the display, Jess peered through its thick metal bars at the creature inside—some kind of huge, coiled snake monster, it seemed. Almost a meter in girth, and with a glistening scaly hide that looked for all the world like chain mail, the creature writhed restlessly in one corner of its cell, massive fanged jaws dripping saliva. A lethal looking spiked fringe ran the length of the monster's spine, while in the center of its squirming body, hinting perhaps at its most recent meal, there was a single, distinctly man-shaped bulge. The cage's glow-in-the-dark sign read:

ARMOURED SHREKSAK
GUARANTEED BULLETPROOF
ALL OFFERS CONSIDERED
CONTACT:
THE BRUCE ~~BROTHERS~~ BROTHER

Jess turned again to Miss Lacey and Sissy. "So... basically, what you're saying is that *all* these animals are sourced from the exact same place? The same place *Sissy* came from? And that said place is somewhere near here?"

"That's precisely what I'm saying," Miss Lacey replied, the gang resuming their trudge through the muddy square. "Not that the town's hunters will be at all inclined to reveal the location of that place though. Hunters' Code, I'm afraid. It's a closely guarded secret."

Jess pondered. "But we can make enquiries?"

"*Discreet* enquiries, yes," Miss Lacey agreed.

"Lady, I *like* your thinking," Sally said, cricking her neck and then slipping on a set of heavy brass knuckle dusters... before double-taking the collection of frowns that came back at her. "What? *Seriously?* 'Discreet enquiries'? That wasn't an ironic euphemism? You people..." and with a disappointed sigh, Sally slipped the knuckle-dusters off again.

As they continued their trek through the square, Jess found herself pausing once more to eye a long parade of darkened shop fronts, the rest of the gang continuing on a step or two while Jess stood there musing. "Does kinda look like everything's shut down for the night," Jess said, scanning for any signs of life behind the broken windows of the business she looked up at:

ASSASIN-NATION
BUY TWO HITS
GET LOWEST VALUE HIT FOR FREE!

But inside the dilapidated shack, not a flicker of lamp or candle was to be seen. "You think maybe we're gonna have to wait till morning?"

Miss Lacey's reply came from just a little way off: "Oh, commerce never sleeps in a place such as this, Ms. Flint. It simply decants to subsidiary premises," and upon turning, Jess saw that the old lady had also come to a stop now, she and the others staring up at the only building in the entire town that appeared to have lights on inside, if dim ones. With the last of the night's grumbling thunder finally fading to silence, Jess was also able to make out sounds coming from inside the rickety wooden structure—the murmur of conversation, the clink of drinks glasses.

Catching up with the rest of the group again, Jess raised her eyes to the building's flaking sign:

THE RUSTY MACHETE SALOON
SYPHILIS FREE SINCE '83

"Lovely," Vera said.

Barring the saloon's filthy swing doors was an equally filthy, broken-toothed bouncer, who stood there in thoughtful silence, chewing on

70

something brown and sticky, substantial quantities of which leaked from one side of his gappy mouth. Set in a face composed largely of bruises and scar tissue, two bloodshot eyes peered down impassively at Jess and co, and after some further thoughtful chewing, the bouncer expelled a golf ball-sized pellet of brown-and-sticky before addressing the hopefuls:

"Sorry, we got a dress code."

Jess and the gang exchanged mystified looks, at a complete loss as to how to respond to this… until the bouncer reached into a large wooden box beside him, hauled out a bunch of guns, gun-belts, and ammo straps, and began handing them out.

"Attractive young party such as yourselves? Can't be too careful," the bouncer said, distributing weapons to Jess, Sally, Vera… before pausing at Dave and subjecting said fella to a more considered scrutiny. "Yeah, *you'll* be fine," the bouncer concluded, dumping the remaining guns back in the box. "In y'all go then, folks. And welcome to the Rusty Machete."

11

The Rusty Machete

Upon entering the Rusty Machete saloon, the first thing that struck Jess did so not through her eyeballs but through her nostrils. If The Town With No Name stank bad on the outside, on the *inside* it smelt like… a truly fitting simile escaped Jess.

But not, of course, Sally: "Sweet Mother McCready, it's like they set up a bar in a sewage worker's butt crack."

And the view wasn't much better either, Jess thought. In the low light of the saloon's handful of oil lamps, shady punters who knew not of this thing called soap clustered at grubby tables, smoking, downing shots, and making deals for smaller caged monsters they'd brought inside with them. All around, the dark mutterings of illegal trade were punctuated with occasional bouts of raucous laughter, while at the feet of each huddled group, the saturated and clumping sawdust on the floor failed to absorb the ongoing trickles of animal waste.

At least, Jess *hoped* it was all just animal waste.

As the saloon's swing doors clattered shut behind Miss Lacey and Sissy in the rearguard of the entering group, Jess fully expected the entire room to go silent and all eyes in the place to spin their way. But nope. Nothing to look at here, it seemed. Which was good.

"Okay," Jess said, turning to the gang, "Dave, with me. The rest of you guys, find us some seats and let's see if we can—"

"Hey, will ya lookit that," Sally interrupted, nodding to a table in a far corner. The table in question was occupied by a lone old man, raggedy and beer-stained, sporting what looked like clumps of vomit in his beard. Not that vomit clumps were in any way noteworthy in a place like the Rusty Machete. What *was* noteworthy however—and what Sal had spotted—was the hunched but muscular form that crouched *next* to the old guy, chained by its neck to an iron ring set in the wall of the saloon. Even in the smoky gloom that permeated the bar, that form, and the silver-gray fur that covered it, were unmistakable.

It was a creature like Sissy.

"Okay, looks promising," Jess said. "You ladies go make enquiries of Mr. Vomit Beard there, and me and Dave will see what we can learn from the management."

"Sounds like a plan," Sally agreed and began to lead the others away, heading for a vacant table next to the old guy and his captive creature.

Alone now with Dave, Jess turned towards the seething mass of grungy punters that lay between them and whatever dubious refreshments might be available in a place such as this. "Right then," Jess said, "so let's go grab us some drinks."

By the time they'd shouldered their way to the length of rutted and bullet-scarred timber that served for a bar in the Rusty Machete, two shot glasses of a dark, oily liquid were already waiting for them, slammed down by a burly, bare-chested bartender who looked like he might have had a profitable showbiz career wrestling great white sharks, if they could have found any great white sharks big enough to be a challenge.

Behind the bar there hung a grubby, hand-scrawled pricelist, along with a sign that read: 'The Management Reserves the Right To Blow Your Goddamn Head Off'. Doing her best to ignore the latter, Jess consulted the former, handed the bartender a couple of bucks, then raised her glass. Beside her, Dave went to follow suit but made the rookie error of sniffing the glass's contents first, gagging instantly like he'd just inhaled something very very dead.

Wheezing out the last of his horror, Dave offered the bartender an apologetic smile. "Um, sorry, you wouldn't, by any chance, happen to have something—" Cue an elbow in the ribs from Jess. "—*stronger,*" Dave concluded hastily. "Something *stronger.*"

The bartender looked Dave up and down, turned away for a moment, then turned back again holding a shot glass filled with an even darker, even oilier liquid. Jess could have sworn she saw actual fumes rising from the stuff—fumes that, had she and Dave been living in a cartoon, would surely have writhed with twisted, demonic faces.

The bartender looked *Jess* up and down now too. "That your rig just rolled in?"

"Yup, that's us," Jess said.

"We're going to the monster hunting grounds tomorrow," Dave put in, mustering a faux cheery grin in the process. "To get us some monsters," he added. And for purposes of ultimate clarity, "Through hunting."

Cringing inwardly, Jess threw Dave a warning look, before turning back to the bartender and indicating her drink. "Gimme three more of these, please, bud."

●●●

As Sally, Miss Lacey, and Sissy stepped up to the vacant table next to Vomit Beard (yes, the nickname appeared to have stuck), Vera, hanging back a little, took advantage of the moment to study the Sissy-like creature chained up by the old man's feet. Only a little smaller than Sissy herself, and with identical silver-gray fur, the animal— very clearly male, Vera could now see—squatted there on his haunches, moaning gently, dark eyes fixed on a regrettably familiar object that dangled from Vomit Beard's belt. Another electric cattle prod. So fearful and intense was the creature's scrutiny of this device that, even as the others began to seat themselves nearby, the monster's gaze did not once shift from it…

… until, that was, Sissy herself moved into his view, whereupon the creature's eyes shot all at once to this female of his species and widened in a near-human look of surprise-cum-astonishment. Thereafter, a new sense of alertness seemed to stiffen the animal's body, and his anguished moan dropped several notches in volume.

Meanwhile, the male creature's hygiene-challenged captor appeared now to be registering his own not insignificant interest in the human contingent of the party settling in 'next door'.

Good, Vera thought. They had gained the man's attention. And sure enough, just as she lowered herself into the last available chair—the one closest to Vomit Beard—the fellow in question leaned over, displaying for Vera's benefit a row of crooked black teeth (or stumps thereof) lurking deep within his soiled and knotted bush of facial hair. Assuming this display to be a smile of some sort, Vera answered it with a polite example of her own, and eventually, on a moist cloud of rampant halitosis, four croaking words emerged from the deeper darkness beyond the man's rot-blackened incisors:

"Looking for breeding opportunities?"

Vera glanced down at Vomit Beard's male creature, then over at Sissy, before directing a questioning look to Sally and Miss Lacey beside her. Both responded with subtle nods of encouragement, and Vera turned once more to Vomit Beard. "Um… breeding opportunities, yes, quite possibly. Do you think they might be a good pairing?"

Vomit Beard returned a lecherous wink. "Weren't talkin 'bout the livestock, sweetie."

"Eeeuw!" and even as Vera's yelp of disgust rang out, Sally's right arm came rocketing past and down, the gal's fingers clamping claw-like onto Vomit Beard's grubby crotch.

"Hands off, pardner," Sally growled, "if'n you

don't want the twins here——" whereupon she proceeded to administer a single hearty squeeze-n-tug, "——to be leavin' home forever. If you get my drift. Please do indicate your assent or otherwise in this matter."

Eyes bulging like they were about to pop, Vomit Beard emitted a single choked whimper and nodded that assent with some considerable fervor, while by his feet, his cowed creature suddenly stopped moaning altogether, now watching all with an intense animal interest.

Releasing Vomit Beard's crotch, a satisfied Sally settled back in her chair, and Vera allowed herself to relax once more… at least until Sally's arm went on to snake its way around Vera's shoulder, where it came to casual rest, Sally's fingers entwining themselves in Vera's hair.

"The gal is mine, bud," Sally said to Vomit Beard, before landing a lingering kiss on Vera's neck. And yes, expedient improv though the move had clearly been on Sally's part, it really was touch and go for a moment whether or not Vera might yelp for a second time tonight—this one a thrilled *"Golly!"* as her heart summersaulted and her neck tingled from the touch of Sally's lips. Fortunately, before Vera could indeed disgrace herself in this way, the third member of their party chose now to enter the scene:

"Please forgive my overly passionate friend,"

Miss Lacey said with an indulgent smile to Sally. "Love makes vengeful serial killers of us all, as they say."

Vomit Beard gulped, stammering, "Um, wh-wh-wh-who says th-th-that, exactly?"

Miss Lacey ignored the question. "*But,*" she continued, "if you were indeed looking to put your rather handsome young fella there out to stud, well then…" and reaching into a shoulder bag, the old lady pulled out a fat wad of cash, allowing the banded stack of twenties to riffle in the light of the table's oil lamp.

At the sight of the cash, Vomit Beard's eyes lit up like two bleary fireworks.

"Of course," Miss Lacey continued, "before we proceed, some information about your creature's background would be *extremely* helpful…"

● ● ●

Please please please, Dave, just shut the hell up, a desperate Jess urged in her head, praying that her eyes didn't betray the spiraling anxiety she felt. *Just this once. You can do it, Dave. I know you can. Yes?*

But no. Even as the bartender was placing the last of the three additional drinks Jess had ordered onto a battered tin tray, Dave continued to blabber blabber blabber to the guy like the bookies' favorite in a blabbering contest:

"I mean it, bro," the fella from Staines went on,

entirely unfazed by the barman's stony silence, "just *so* damn busy, know what I'm saying? Hunter's work ain't never done, am I right? I mean, what with all the *hunting* and stuff."

"Dave," Jess muttered under her breath, "you really need to——"

"Caught us a live Klingon last week."

"Oh, god…"

"Prob'ly ain't heard of them, right? Mars Bar foreheads and a real bad attitude. Good mark up to the right buyer, mind," and here Dave worked in a strategic pause, followed by a fake sip at his drink, then, finally, the moment he'd clearly been maneuvering his way towards for the last three excruciating minutes: "So, anyhoo, as I say, been a while since we been up at the ol' hunting grounds round here. Think you could remind us how we——"

"Go home, kids," the bartender said.

Aaaaand there it was at last. The shutting up.

"Excuse me?" Dave managed, in response to which the bartender leaned forward, fixing both Dave and Jess with the very darkest of scowls:

"I *said,* go home. Cos I promise you, between here and the grounds? Biggest mess of unmapped railroad on the whole of Mars. Smarter crews than you have tried to find 'em. Smarter crews than you ain't never been seen again. So I repeat——" The bartender shoved the drinks-filled tray at Jess and, against all odds, succeeded in squeezing just a shade more darkness out of his scowl. "—finish your refreshments and *go home.*"

●●●

While Miss Lacey and Vomit Beard continued their negotiations across the two grimy tables, Vera let her attention drift back to the male creature chained to the wall beside them. The poor thing was once again moaning balefully, although Vera couldn't help but note a distinct and curious difference in the attitude that accompanied these vocalizations now: through them all, the creature's dark and pain-filled eyes remained fixed not on the electric cattle prod that hung from Vomit Beard's belt but on Sissy.

For her part, Sissy appeared reluctant to return the male creature's gaze and kept her head lowered, but this seemed in no way to deter the other animal, who continued to study his female counterpart with a profound curiosity, cocking his shaggy head at the dress Sissy wore and cultivating an expression that, to Vera at least, looked a whole lot like puzzlement.

"Do you really need to keep him chained up like that?" Vera asked Vomit Beard, interrupting the ongoing negotiations.

"Ha! Damn right!" the man barked in response. "Fresh from the tree, this fella. One sniff of

81

freedom and he'd be back there by morning."

At the sound of the man's raised voice, the male creature shrank into himself and moaned louder, the plaintive tone of it cutting straight to Vera's heart.

Not to Vomit Beard's though. "Jeez, boy," the man snarled, "would ya plug yer hole!"

At Vera's shoulder, Miss Lacey leaned in and *ahem-ed* politely, smiling at Vomit Beard then tapping her pencil on the pad she'd been using to take notes. "So, yes, these 'hunting grounds' you mentioned? How exactly does one get there?"

"Ha! Nice try, lady," Vomit Beard came back, raising a lone you-can't-fool-me finger and grinning coyly. "You know the rules. Hunters *only*."

"Oh, please," Miss Lacey scoffed. "Bureaucratic piffle. Nobody need know you even told us," and not for the first time in these negotiations, the old lady's eyes traveled to the bulging wad of money on the table, Vomit Beard's own eyes duly following, drinking in the cash…

"It's really just for our records," Miss Lacey added with an innocuous smile.

After another moment, Vomit Beard raised his eyes again and glanced about nervously, as if checking to see whether anyone in the bar was watching. At the same time, the creature at his feet gave out another moan, louder this time. Longer too.

"Dammit, boy," Vomit Beard snapped at the animal, "would you shut the hell up and just let me *think* here."

As the man continued to ponder, Vera looked up to see Jess and Dave approaching from the bar, but apparently sensing that negotiations might be at a critical juncture, the pair drew to a discreet stop just a couple of steps shy of the table, where they stood in silence, waiting.

Once again, Miss Lacey offered Vomit Beard her innocent, old-lady smile. "Well?" she said, and for another second or two, the tense silence stretched on.

But then, at last, Vomit Beard nodded and smiled back, opening his mouth as if about to answer. Unfortunately, before that answer could emerge, the creature at the old man's feet chose the same moment to let out yet another moan—this one louder still, *longer* still—and that, it seemed, was the final straw.

Whirling on the monster, Vomit Beard hauled his electric cattle prod from its holster, yelled, "Boy, did I not just *warn* you?" and jammed the device into the chained and crouching animal. Sparks flew, smoke rose, and the creature roared in agony, all eyes in the saloon turning at the sound.

"Oi! What the hell!" Dave bellowed. "Out of

order, man!" and with his eyes flashing in rage, the boy from Staines threw himself forward, shouldering Vomit Beard to the floor and wrenching the cattle prod from the guy's grasp.

"Hey!" a furious Vomit Beard yelled back, clambering to his feet and lunging for Dave, while at the same time, Sissy leapt roaring from her chair and onto Vomit Beard's table, her fists raised high, ready to pound, ready to—

But then, cutting through the clamor, there came a single, heart-stopping sound—the unmistakable CLICK of a gun hammer being cocked.

"Enough," a gravel voice intoned, and Vera whirled with the others to see a towering, bare-chested figure standing behind Dave.

It was the bartender, and clutched in the man's raised right hand was a revolver the size of a small cannon.

12

And Sal Thought Her Plans Were Crazy

Jess froze, her heart thudding as the bartender stepped forward, yanked the cattle prod from a fear-paralyzed Dave, and tossed the thing to Vomit Beard. Glowering in fury, the old monster hunter immediately raised the device to Sissy on the table, who, with a whimper of terror, fell back at once, dropping to the floor and scurrying into Miss Lacey's arms.

A dead silence fell on the saloon.

"Okay, so who the hell are you really?" the bartender growled at Jess and her friends, the muzzle of his outsize six-shooter sweeping the silent group. "Police? IRS? Animal Liberation?"

Sissy whimpered again, louder this time, and Jess saw the barman's face twist in disgust as Miss Lacey comforted the terrified creature.

"Aw, Jeezus," the bartender spat. "Frickin critter lovers…"

Ten seconds later, after being stripped of their 'house' weaponry, Jess, Vera, Sally, Miss Lacey, and Sissy, were ejected en masse from the Rusty Machete—thrust through its rickety swing doors, bundled over the bullet-pocked stoop, and flung out into the filth-strewn street beyond.

"Chin up, gang," Sally said as they all stumbled to a stop in the mud and turned to stare back at the saloon. "Take it from a gal who knows, there's worse ways to be kicked outta bars," whereupon the building's lone intact window pane exploded in a shower of glass as Dave came cannoning through it to land face down in the squalor. "One of them right there," Sally observed.

Framed in the broken window, the bartender stood blowing on his fist, scowling at them all for a moment more until, with a final look of contempt, he turned and swaggered back into the saloon.

Dashing forward with the others to help Dave, Jess grabbed the fella's left arm and, together with Sally and Vera, extracted him from the mud with a sucking squelch. "You okay?" Jess asked.

"I'll live," Dave said, before adding, somewhat

shamefaced, "Sorry about that. It's just... the old guy was hurting him. I couldn't let—"

"I know," Jess said. "I get it. And once again, 'the right thing'. Proper Prince Valiant, you're turning out to be this trip," in response to which Dave mustered a weak but grateful smile.

As a mewling Sissy stepped in to help Dave scrape the mud from his overalls, Jess turned to the others. "It does leave us with a bit of a problem though. Cos no way is anyone in there gonna show us where the hunting grounds are now. No way in hell." Expecting a spell of thoughtful silence to follow this grim assessment, Jess was surprised when Vera spoke up almost immediately:

"Actually," the gal said, "that may not be *entirely* true," and on turning to question her English friend, Jess was further surprised to encounter a pair of eyes that already twinkled with what could only be inspiration. "No, that may not be true at all," Vera mused...

•••

A mere twenty minutes on from mooting her idea to the rest of the gang, Vera Middleton stood peering through the half-open back door of the Rusty Machete, a growing tension clawing at her stomach. Because with the largely preparatory Phase One of the plan having gone swiftly and without a hitch, the prospect of the rather more unpleasant Phase Two now loomed, and loomed *large.* Indeed, by Vera's reckoning, the terrible thing that was about to happen in the crowded saloon could surely be only seconds away. A minute at most.

She was not wrong.

As Vera watched through the doorway, she saw the bartender serve up one last shot of liquor to a teetering, cross-eyed customer, and then, even as the barman yanked a crumpled banknote from the drunkard's hand, it began.

Vera didn't actually *hear* that first THUMP, just saw the bartender's reaction to it, his eyes darting in confusion to the floor behind the bar.

The *second* THUMP though? That was *easily* loud enough for Vera to pick up above the bustle of the packed saloon. And loud enough to make the bartender leap back in shock, his eyes shooting again to the floor at his feet.

There was no third THUMP. Instead, what came next was one almighty CRASH as the huge armored snake creature from the cage in the town square—a *shreksak,* Vera reminded herself—burst through the bar-side cellar trapdoor and surged up onto the counter.

Chaos erupted instantly. Screaming customers began to race for exits—upending tables, shouldering slower punters aside, trampling others into the floor. A handful of random gunshots rang out, and Vera's heart leapt at the sound, ear-shattering in the enclosed environment. As far as she could tell though, most of the shots went wide, while the few that *did* find their mark ricocheted uselessly off the shreksak's armored hide.

"Oh, golly…" Vera said, directing a wide-eyed glance at the two figures who stood behind her: Dave, similarly agog at the shrieking mayhem visible through the saloon's back door; and Sally, grinning at it all with dark delight from the pilot's seat of her steam-loader exo-skeleton. As the mechanical muscle behind the entire plan, the huge steam-powered robot suit—Sally's pride and joy—was what had made such short work of Phase One, dragging the shreksak's cage from the town square, releasing the furious creature into the saloon's streetside cellar trapdoor, and then leaving the thing to be drawn to the ripe smells of the packed saloon above it. The entire procedure had been the work of mere minutes, an enthusiastic Sally clearly relishing both it *and* the spectacular Phase Two consequences they were all now observing.

Vera, however, continued to have grave concerns—both for the poor used-and-abused shreksak as well as for its potential victims, lowlives though they might be. "Oh, golly," she said again, wincing as the snake creature lunged at a cluster of terrified customers crammed into a toilet doorway, "it's not really going to devour someone in there, is it?"

"Relax," Sally drawled, stooping to get herself a better view through the half-open door. "Like the old lady said, thing clearly just ate. Ain't gonna need another meal for months."

Inside the saloon, the screaming and crashing surged to still more cacophonous heights, and Sally turned to Dave. "Okay, now or never, dude," she said, upon which Dave returned a steely-eyed nod, shoved the saloon's back door fully open, and dived inside.

Head down, eyes darting left and right, the boy from Staines wove his way through the howling madness the Rusty Machete had fallen into, while at the other end of the room, the shreksak continued its hissing, snapping rampage, crashing through tables and chairs, battering into walls, lunging for anyone unfortunate enough to get too close.

Several heart-in-mouth seconds later, goggle-eyed and out of breath, Dave arrived at his destination—Vomit Beard's table in the corner—where, just as they had all suspected would be the case (and making things a whole lot easier for Dave), the old man was nowhere to be seen, having fled the danger without even bothering to free his helpless captive. Still chained to the saloon

90

wall, the abandoned creature roared and thrashed in the surrounding bedlam, hauling in vain at his bonds.

Crouched low, and hidden by the ongoing uproar, Dave pulled a pair of heavy-duty wire-cutters from a bag slung over his shoulder and quickly cut the chain shackling the creature to the wall. It was at that point that the monster seemed finally to become aware of the human beside him and whirled with a shriek of fury, raising his fists high, ready to pound.

Watching from the doorway, Vera gasped, her heart lurching.

But then the creature paused, a tilt of his shaggy head seeming to communicate a startled, if confused, recognition of what Dave had just done.

For one more excruciating moment, the monster stood there, staring back at Dave… and then the pair of them were up and gone, Dave leading the charge for the saloon's back door.

Well okay then, Vera thought. Now for *her* part in the plan.

As Dave and the creature barreled towards the open door, Vera stepped aside and grabbed the metal cannister at her feet. A split-second later, wide-eyed with terror, Dave came flying through the exit, and faced with the screeching nightmare of fur and fangs that followed him, Vera felt her every muscle turn to jelly. "I am *so* sorry about this," she said to the creature—

—before throwing the entire contents of the metal cannister—four slopping liters of glow-in-the-dark paint—straight at the silvery-gray figure as it hurtled through the doorway.

Just as Vera had known it would, much of the paint simply went splattering to the ground by the saloon door, but a significant quantity of the stuff did also find its target, coating the fleeing creature with a top-to-toe splash of brilliant white, and a few steps on, the monster skidded to a stop, turning to look back at Vera in clear bewilderment—

—before once again roaring his fury and charging off across the town square.

It was then that something entirely unexpected happened.

When they'd talked the whole plan through, the presumption had been that, at this point, the monster would simply race away into the night.

But he didn't.

Instead, the creature paused, sniffed at the air… and then abruptly changed direction, heading full tilt for the Cannonball Express, still in its siding on the far side of the square.

By the rear of the train, clamping her steam-loader back onto its flatbed, Sally looked up to see the creature charging towards her and dropped hastily into a defensive stance.

But no, the animal ignored Sally, galloping straight on past without so much as a glance and heading farther up the train.

"Huh?" Dave said to Vera. "What the hell is he doing?"

Seconds later, the paint-splattered monster arrived at the crew car, gave out a single piercing howl, and then leapt up to cling ape-like to the carriage's bullet-riddled side, peering in its sole un-boarded-up window. Vera could see a startled Sissy and Miss Lacey on the opposite side of the glass, huddled together in a window seat, and as the male creature locked eyes with his female opposite number, Sissy shrieked in fear then darted backwards, disappearing with Miss Lacey into the shadows farther inside.

The male creature roared. Roared again. But neither Sissy nor Miss Lacey reappeared at the window, and eventually, after one final roar, the monster dropped to the ground, turned on his heels, and raced away.

With the plan apparently heading back on track, Vera heaved a sigh of relief, and even as the sound of it escaped her lips, the shrill blast of a steam whistle pierced the night air, Vera's gaze darting to the *front* of the train now—to the Cannonball itself, in whose cab a frantic Jess stood yanking on the whistle chain while smoke from the engine billowed around her.

"Okay," Vera said to Dave beside her, "let's go," and together the pair of them bolted for the loco, covering the twenty meters of muddy town square in seconds then hauling themselves up into the cab with Jess.

Her steam-loader now stowed and secure, Sally was right behind them, and even as the gal's boots hit the footplate, Jess's hands went to work—a whirlwind of motion as she released the brake, cranked a half dozen valves and levers, and worked the Cannonball's throttle. In response, the locomotive gave a rumble, a lurch, and moments later, accompanied by a deafening blast of steam, the train was off, accelerating out of the siding at a rate only their supercharged-by-alien-technology engine could hope to achieve.

Shooting a glance behind her through a side window, Vera caught one last glimpse of the rampaging shreksak as it burst shrieking from the Rusty Machete to slither off into the night, and then, just seconds after that, The Town With No Name was gone, the entire filth-ridden excuse for a settlement lost in darkness as the Cannonball Express, plus its full complement of crew, passengers, and rolling stock, thundered away in a cloud of smoke and steam and red Martian dust.

"Vera, you're with Sal," Jess barked, and pulling her head back into the cab, Vera snapped to it, following Sally up through the cab's roof hatch and into the gunner's compartment above. Because of course, none of this would mean a thing if they couldn't actually *see* the male creature to follow him back to the hunting grounds.

Dropping into position behind the loco's laser cannon, Vera grabbed the binoculars that were stashed there, while in the seat adjacent, Sally grabbed a second pair of the same and turned to the voice tube horn, addressing Jess and Dave in the cab below:

"Gotta say though, people, über kudos to our V here. Glow-in-the-dark paint and a homing werewolf? And I thought *my* plans were crazy ass."

Vera cheeks burned with a hot blend of joy, pride, and embarrassment.

"I take it you got eyes on the prize then?" Jess's voice came back, loud and clear over the voice tube's brass horn.

"We have indeed," Vera answered, because yes, there he was in her binoculars, his galloping ape-like form maybe a hundred meters ahead of the speeding Cannonball, paint-splattered fur glowing bright in the darkness.

In the end, it had been the region's geography—with its flat, barren plains stretching all the way to the horizon—that had sealed the deal. That had persuaded the gang to take a chance on what was, Vera would freely admit, something of an 'out there' plan. Said geography, along with the prospect of an unusually clear Martian night ahead, had suggested that the chances of keeping the creature in sight for long stretches were at least *reasonably* good. And if what the bartender had told Jess about the density of legacy railworks in the region proved true, finding suitable tracks to keep the Cannonball on the monster's tail might not be as big an ask as it sounded. Was it a gamble? For sure. A *big* gamble. But in the absence of any less 'crazy ass' plan, it had, they'd all agreed, been a gamble worth taking.

"Okay, here we go, people," Vera said as the creature ahead of them veered suddenly to the left, away from the single track the Cannonball rode. Fortunately, Vera could already see a suitable junction just a little farther on, its railside points lever caught in the yellow glow of the loco's headlamp

"Vera's right," Sally barked into the voice tube. "Hit the brakes, babe. We need to take the *westerly* track," and moments later, the train began to slow, in preparation for the first of who knew how many sudden and erratic direction changes they might eventually have to make on this ever more outlandish excursion.

13

Tough Crowd

Yosemite Sam! That's who this fella reminded Slinger of! Gosh-darned Yosemite Sam! If the god-like genius known to history as Friz Freleng had seen fit to paint some vomit onto that venerable cartoon character's red beard, maybe blacken out a few of his toony teeth, why then, gosh-darned spitting image is what Slinger humbly opined. The thought made him laugh out loud.

Not that the real-life fella in question—currently dangling by the neck from Slinger's uppermost left hand—saw the funny side.

And neither, it would seem, did the remainder of the befouled and reeking clientele in this cesspool of a drinking hole, every last one of whom looked on in grim silence, radiating malicious intent like Wile E. Coyote unboxing his latest delivery from the Acme Corporation.

"Swear to god, mister, I *cain't* tell ya that," Yosemite Sam whined (shame he didn't have the voice). "I just *cain't*. Hunters only, know what I'm sayin'? I've told you everything I——"

From the corner of one eye, Slinger caught several flickers of movement as a number of the Rusty Machete's more incautious customers went for their weapons. In the proverbial flash, the full complement of Slinger's unoccupied hands flew into motion, whipping five of his six revolvers from their mother-of-pearl encrusted holsters. As ever, the near supernatural speed of Slinger's multi-gun draw stopped every last one of his would be assailants in their tracks. Their *profoundly soiled* tracks, Slinger's unhappy brain added. Darn it all, but if there was one thing he hated more than cursing, it was poor personal hygiene.

"Hmmm," Slinger mused in the dead silence that followed. "Seems to me that you good folks might require something in the nature of an instructive demonstration," and with Yosemite Sam still choking in his fist, Slinger re-aimed one of his six-shooters at the nearest of the saloon's glass-free windows, currently framed in which was the lone figure of Slinger's ex-wife, lounging against the porch rail outside. A tiny stub of cigar protruded from Zora's lips, and as Slinger's single gunshot rang out, that same stub duly vanished in a puff of ash and a mini explosion of shredded tobacco.

In the saloon, an audible gasp from the Rusty Machete's frozen clientele, along with the even deeper silence that followed it, told Slinger everything he needed to know about the 'instructiveness' of his demonstration. All present were, without a shadow of a doubt, *powerfully* impressed.

Zora, on the other hand…

Rolling her eyes with calculated disdain, the woman simply pulled another fat cigar from a fancy silver case and drawled, "For the love of god, Zab, would you get *on* with it. Do we or do we not have the information we need?"

Slinger sighed. "Yes, Zora, I believe we do," and with his five drawn weapons covering his retreat, Slinger hauled Yosemite Sam backwards across the floor of the saloon, then on through its swing doors.

Outside, Zora was already lighting up a replacement smoke, and even as she drew from it a first rasping lungful, she rose, stepped off the porch, and began to head across the filth-strewn square of The Town With No Name.

Dragging a now silent and compliant Yosemite

with him, Slinger followed, his five drawn revolvers aimed backwards over his shoulders at the saloon's exit. Okay, for sure, chances (sadly) were that no one would be fool enough to make a move now. But hey, you never knew, right?

Halfway across the square, Slinger risked some light conversation. "Just like the old days, huh, Zora?" he said, nodding to the cigar the woman continued to pull on.

"In the old days, I don't recall our audiences being quite so murderous," a stony-faced Zora replied, whereupon, with a clatter of bootheels and a cacophony of curses, a mob of gun-toting punters erupted from the saloon behind, prompting Slinger's five backward pointing Colt 45s to loose a storm of lead over both shoulders. Seconds later, a dozen or more fresh corpses lay decorating the dirt in front of the Rusty Machete.

"What can I say? Tough crowd," Slinger conceded. "So anyways, Sam here"—he prodded Yosemite in the back with the muzzle of one still smoking gun—"tells me they got maybe half a day's start. Goin' slow though, seein' as how their guide is on foot."

"On *foot?*" Zora raised an intrigued eyebrow.

"Tell ya later. Let's move it. They are *not* gettin' away again."

"No, Zab, they most certainly are not. Especially not now the *cavalry's* here," and finally arriving at the far side of the town square, Zora drew to a stop with Slinger, the pair of them looking up to admire the aforementioned 'cavalry' in all its coal-fired glory.

The show train stood parked in a siding that ran adjacent to the square—the same siding the Flint gal had apparently parked her own ride in last night, Slinger had learned—and presented, as ever, an eye-popping spectacle against the muted reddish-browns of the Martian landscape. Behind the powerful, sixteen-wheeler loco, the company's mixed rolling stock—crew cars, sleepers, freight wagons, a laden flatbed or ten—shone with color in the noonday sun, the principal source of that color being the legend, in gaudy letters almost three meters high, that ran the length of the entire train: 'PETROVNA'S FAMOUS CARNIVAL OF MARS'. To Slinger, the whole thing looked, as it always had, like something out of a Loony Tunes cartoon. Needless to say, a singularly pleasing appearance in the eyes of western Mars's foremost enforcer-for-hire.

Zora waved to the locomotive's driver, currently standing by the footplate and gawping in mute shock at the body strewn ground in front of the Rusty Machete.

"Fire her up, Joe," Zora called over to the man, who, most unwisely in Slinger's humble opinion, remained frozen and agog for several more seconds, before blurting out:

"Mother of god, Zora, what the *hell* was—"

"I said *fire her up!*" Zora snapped at the fella, adopting one of those defy-me-and-you-lose-your-man-parts looks she seemed to have mastered sometime in early girlhood.

And yup, that did it. The fella called Joe gulped, nodded, hauled himself up into the engine's cab, and began yanking the controls.

Zora took one last moment to beam at the other shocked faces in the windows of the train's several crew cars then yelled, "Okay, folks, we are moving out!" following which words a deafening blast of steam exploded from the loco's pistons.

"Damn, but I love show business," Zora added by way of an appropriate exit line and then stepped aboard the train.

14

A Big Hairy Mirror

"I certainly couldn't claim to be any kind of creature trainer, no," Miss Lacey said, her liver-spotted fingers working away at her knitting again. "Believe it or not, I was *actually* the company's business manager. Not really show people at all, and in no way experienced in the care of animals, let alone an animal such as Sissy."

Huddled in a corner seat of the crew car while the Cannonball rumbled ever farther north through a bright Martian afternoon, Miss Lacey was beginning to looked tired, Jess thought. Both physically *and* emotionally. And who could blame her?

"So how come she ended up with you then?" Jess asked.

"Pure luck, really," the old lady said. "At the time the company first got her, there just happened to be a spare bunk in my cabin, and Zora thought it might help with Sissy's general domestication, so…" She paused, gulping a little before continuing. "Sixteen years, Ms. Flint. *Sixteen years* we've been together, Sissy and I…" Miss Lacey laid down her knitting to dab at her welling eyes. "I'm sorry, you'll have to forgive me. I never had children of my own, so all of this…" She drew in a long wavery breath. "I suppose it just took me a little by surprise."

Laying a hand on the woman's arm, Jess offered her passenger a smile of support, and after another shaky breath, the old lady nodded her appreciation then picked up her knitting once more.

As the soft clickety-clack of Miss Lacey's knitting needles resumed, Jess shifted her attention to Sally, the gal no longer up top in the loco's gun turret but perched in a seat halfway down the crew car, her head stuck out what was now the car's sole unbroken, un-boarded up window. While the move to below had come as something of a surprise, Sally had made it with a deal of confidence, she and Vera agreeing to abandon their previous lookout post shortly after dawn when it had become clear to all that keeping

104

eyes on the male creature would actually be a lot easier than any of them had anticipated.

"Our boy still there then, Sal?" Jess called over.

"Uh-huh," Sally answered, "sure is. I swear again though, babe, ain't like it's us following him at all now. More like him *leading us.*"

"Which makes absolutely *no* sense."

"Yeah, well, tell that to Butch," Sally replied, having by now, of course, named the hairy fella in question. "Come and see for yourself if you don't believe me."

Stepping in behind Sally, Jess thrust her own head out the window, and sure enough, there was 'Butch' in all his silver-gray, paint-splattered glory, still bounding along ahead of the Cannonball while shooting the occasional glance back over his shoulder, as if to check the train was still following. It really was a puzzler, Jess thought. Even the many junctions they were forced to negotiate in this spaghetti of exploratory rail routes were proving to be little problem—every time they had to stop and shift some points in order to follow the creature's change of direction, Butch would take immediate note, pause helpfully where he was, wait till the job was done, and then simply gallop on as before, with the Cannonball on his tail again.

"Nope. Makes no sense *at all,*" Jess repeated.

"Hmmm," came Miss Lacey's voice from

behind, "I think it *might* actually…"

Together, Jess and Sally pulled their heads back into the carriage and exchanged baffled frowns. Then two seconds later, the penny dropped for both of them. "Sissy," they said in unison.

"Sissy," Miss Lacey confirmed. "I rather suspect my not-so-little girl may have caught that young fellow's eye, don't you think?"

Now that the idea had been put out there, Jess did indeed think. It was the only possible explanation, and frankly, Jess was amazed she hadn't seen it herself until this moment.

"Talking of Her Hairiness," Sally said, "dare I suggest conspicuous by her absence?"

"Last I saw her she was poking around the crew cabins," Jess replied.

Miss Lacey smiled and nodded. "Yes, she is a bit of a curious one, I'm afraid. But don't worry. I'm sure she'll be fine."

Just then, the door at the forward end of the carriage clattered open, and a sweaty, soot-stained Dave came trudging in. Heaving out the weary sigh of someone who'd just spent the last two hours shoveling coal, the fella slumped into the nearest chair and tipped Sally a nod.

"Yeah yeah, I'm on it," Sally came back, rising and pulling on her overalls even as Dave began to unbuckle his own mucky footwear.

"And Jess, you might wanna relieve Vera too,"

Dave said, hauling off his work boots and tossing them into a corner. "She's looking kinda past it."

Jess smiled and rolled her eyes. "Yeah, well, the way you been working the gal between shifts, I'm not surprised. Maybe rest those dancing feet this time round, huh?"

"Actually," Miss Lacey put in, "you might not have to."

Dave looked up, confused. "Sorry?"

"Skip dance practice, I mean," Miss Lacey said.

At first, Jess had no idea what the old lady was getting at, and both Dave and Sally looked equally mystified. But then, upon following Miss Lacey's gaze—currently directed over Dave's left shoulder—all became clear. Well, to Jess and Sally anyway.

Dave himself, seated as he was with his back to the door the new arrival had entered through, took a little longer to cotton on, but in the end, a growl from behind got the fella leaping to his feet, whirling on his heels—

—and there she was. Her Hairy Highness herself.

And hoo boy, did the creature not present a perfect, if unexpected, picture.

"What the *hell?*" Sally blurted. "Is that my Parisian one hundred percent silk?" and while herself no expert in such matters, Jess concluded nonetheless that it surely must be.

Poised fully upright before a speechless Dave, her arms raised in a graceful ballroom hold position, Sissy stood there draped in one of Sally's most dazzling show dresses (the 'Rose of Tranquility' always traveled with a theatrical costume or two, "just in case," as she would somewhat vaguely put it by way of justification). Unzipped at the back and bagging around Sissy's upper torso, the frock did at least appear undamaged, Jess noted with relief, while moreover—and here, possibly, was the biggest surprise of all—the fancy, lace-trimmed creation seemed *actually* to be a not unreasonable fit for the essentially human-sized creature it now clothed.

"She's been through my *stuff?*" Sally gasped in disbelief.

"Oh, my goodness, I am so *so* sorry," Miss Lacey said, bustling towards Sissy. "She never could resist anything in silk. Sissy, take that off at once. It's not—"

But then, as the old lady reached for the frilly shoulders of the sagging ballgown, Sally took a step forward and placed a hand on Miss Lacey's arm. "Actually," Sal said, a thoughtful cast settling over her pin-up perfect features, "you know what? It's cool."

"Um… really?" Miss Lacey replied. "Are you sure?"

"Can't quite believe I'm saying this," Sally

mused, "but… the gal *kind* of pulls it off," and cocking her head in deeper thought still, she took a single tentative step towards the creature—

—who whirled in Sally's direction and let out a dangerous growl, her elegant ballroom posture arching instantly into one of feral aggression.

"Relax, sister," Sally said, pausing with her hands raised in submission. "Here to help."

And to Jess's surprise, the gesture did in fact appear to placate the animal, who cocked her own head now, that arch of tension departing her slim but muscular frame.

After another moment, Sally stepped forward again, moved in behind Sissy, and gently removed the creature's coal scuttle bonnet. This done, she began to hand comb Sissy's shoulder-length hair, and it was at that point that Jess was struck by something she hadn't noticed before: down one side of the creature's otherwise silver-gray tresses, previously hidden by her bonnet, there was a long single streak of silky black, its deep and lustrous darkness dotted with eye-catching flecks of pure white, like a slow-moving river reflecting a starry night sky.

Registering the distinctive marking herself, Sally smiled. "Nice. Gal could pay good money for a fancy highlight like that," she said, the observation followed by a startled, "*Whoah!*" as Sally then recoiled a little, eyes widening. "And is that my *Passion by Elizabeth Taylor?*"

It certainly was. Jess could smell the perfume from halfway across the carriage.

Sally's smile grew wider. "*Damn,* babe," she said to Sissy, "but you mean *business.*"

With the creature's hair now apparently arranged to Ms. Chu's satisfaction, Sally nodded, reached down for the dress's zip, yanked it up in one swift motion, and, in a final move of sisterly solidarity, leaned forward to whisper in Sissy's ear, "Go get him, girl."

Turning once more to Dave, Sissy resumed her graceful ballroom hold position, and Jess was almost certain she saw just a dash of extra confidence in the creature's poised frame.

Dave, meanwhile, continued simply to stand there, speechless and at a complete loss.

"Don't be afraid," Miss Lacey said to him. "Granted, she *is* more of a ballet girl really, but she was always a quick study. And she *has* been watching *very* carefully."

During these words of encouragement from the old lady, a grinning Jess had surreptitiously lifted the lid of the gramophone in the corner of the crew car and given its winding handle a few quick turns. With the turntable now spinning as a result, Jess lowered the record player's arm onto the shellac disc, and following a brief crackle of groove noise, a bright and breezy foxtrot began to play.

But still Dave made no move. Just stood there in wide-eyed bewilderment, trembling visibly. Eventually, a few words did make their way out of the fella's slack mouth. Not many, and not in an order that made immediate sense, but, hey, words nonetheless:

"I... what I... do I..." he said. "Does she... want me to... lead or—"

Lunging forward, Sissy grabbed Dave by the waist and, with a distinctly passionate growl, hauled him hard into her erect body.

"Nope," Dave whimpered, "apparently not..." and then they were off down the aisle of the crew car, Sissy leading the dance with a quite startling assurance, Dave responding with the kind of performance you might anticipate from a fella who finds himself unexpectedly foxtrotting with a monster in a ball gown.

"Seriously," Sally said, her smile wider than ever, her voice tinged with a new respect, "it's like looking in a big hairy mirror."

15

Leaves on the Line

Even over the clank and clatter of the Cannonball's engine, a perpetual rhythmic symphony in the loco's cab, Jess could hear the distant cry of the creature they followed—the creature they were all now calling Butch. Back again at the throttle, with Sally by her side stoking the boiler, Jess shot a look through the cab's forward window, and sure enough, there the hairy fella was, perched on an overhang of rock above a narrow pass between two sheer, towering cliff faces. Beating at his chest and howling to the blue sky above, the creature stood there like the Werewolf King of Mars, the high-toned sound of his cry echoing across the mountainous, un-terraformed region they'd come to on the far side of the flat plains that had marked the start of their journey with Butch.

Un-terraformed. And *there* was the confusing word in that sentence, Jess thought. Because yes, while the landscape here certainly *looked* un-terraformed—bleak, rocky terrain? Check. No signs of life whatsoever? Check—when Jess examined her wristband air monitor, its display panel continued to show a solid green, as it had done for close to half an hour now. What's more, Jess's own lungs—Sally's too—appeared to confirm the device's positive reading. Normally, when traveling through a Free Zone, breathers were all but mandatory for the Cannonball's driver and fireman, the rear side of the cab being open to both the elements and the atmosphere. For at least the last sixty kilometers though, neither Jess nor Sally had felt even the slightest need for the respirator devices. And it wasn't just *good* air they were breathing here, it was *great* air. So much so that Jess had even turned off the oxygen supply they normally pumped to the train's enclosed crew and passenger areas. All of which begged the question: just what the hell could be filtering the atmospheric toxins and generating oxygen way out here, several hundred kilometers distance from the nearest official air-production plant?

Chewing on her lip in puzzlement, Jess shot a further look through the cab's forward window...

... and paused, noting with interest that the towering cliff face ahead of them—the one with the pass the Cannonball would shortly steam its way through—seemed in fact to be the crumbling rim of a single gigantic crater. It was only now they were closer to the formation that Jess could discern this clearly, and see also just how immense the thing actually was—quite possibly the highest such crater rim Jess had ever encountered on Mars. As for the vast circular area the full crater must have enclosed? Enough to drop a good-sized Martian city in. Easily. Impressive, Jess mused, and turned to Sally to say so.

Unfortunately, Sally being Sally, Jess never got the chance to broach the subject, the irritating Ms. Chu being determined still to pursue another topic entirely—a topic Jess had been trying in vain to maneuver her way out of for the last ten minutes.

"Seriously though," Sally said, "he *is* kinda sweet, yes? In a never-been-kissed-cos-I'm-such-a-total-sci-fi-geek sorta way."

Jess sighed. "Oh, come on, Sal? You too? Did Vera put you up to this?"

On either side of the cab, vertical rockface filled the loco's windows as the Cannonball entered the narrow pass in the crater rim.

"All I'm saying," Sally continued, "hot babe in

oil-stained denims, sweet guy with underemployed winky. I am visualizing serious passion here, hon. Romeo and Julianne stuff."

"*Et*. Juli*et*. And *stop* visualizing."

"Too late. There's grease guns now too. Also a sheepskin rug. Pray it's machine-washable."

"Look, even if Dave *was* into me, and even if I was into him——"

"What? Big Blonde and Irish?" Sally said. *Scoffed,* even. "And how exactly does *he* love thee, babe? Let me count the ways. None. None ways. Three months and not a single letter."

Jess shook her head in exasperation. Also, if she were being honest, *anger*. Because in the end, Sally was right, dammit. At the time, Jess had been all but certain that Big Blonde and Irish—otherwise known as Declan Donavan, otherwise known as not-a-single-frickin-letter-in-three-frickin-months—was attracted to her. Even Sally had thought so. *Now* though… Okay, sure, so Jess *could* have written to *him*. No law against that. But she hadn't. Had decided instead to let Declan make the first move. Why? Fear of looking desperate? Basic insecurity? Who the hell knew? And now…

Another echoing howl from Butch dragged Jess out of her thoughts, and more than glad of a distraction from these uncomfortable questions, she raised her chin to direct a further glance through the loco's forward window—

—only to freeze in utter astonishment, her eyes wide, her mind reeling.

"Oh…" she finally managed. "Oh wow…"

"Ha!" Sally said, jamming another shovelful of coal into the firebox. "*You're* visualizing it *too* now, ain'tcha? Grease guns, sheepskin rug…"

"What? No. I *meant…* oh *wow…*" and raising a single finger, Jess pointed through the cab's forward window to what lay ahead.

Frowning, Sally turned to look herself… and then she froze too, her jaw dropping like an unlatched tailgate. "Okaaaay," the gal said eventually, "gonna see your *oh wow* and raise you a *holy crap…*"

Because with the Cannonball now emerging from the other end of the narrow pass, what had previously been hidden from Jess and Sal behind the crater's towering wall finally stood revealed.

It was a tree.

But not just any tree. Oh, lordy, no.

The breathtaking organism that loomed before Jess and Sally, close to the very center of the crater's epic bowl, was what surely had to be the single biggest tree in the entire galaxy. From its vast trunk (easily half a kilometer in diameter, Jess estimated) sprouted boughs as broad as the Empire State, branches as wide as freeways, while dangling from the ends of 'twigs' thick enough to be trees in their own right, leaves the size of baseball diamonds rippled in the breeze, gleaming a deep waxy green in the late afternoon sun.

And the heart-stopping spectacle of it all did *not* end there. Because up this truly mind-boggling specimen of nature-gone-crazy, supported by an absurdly complex web of rusting steelwork, there wound a railroad. Single-track and apparently standard gauge, the two parallel rails spiraled their way around the circumference of the gigantic tree, vanishing occasionally behind foliage, but emerging again a little farther up, until they arrived at what appeared to be some kind of building, shrouded in fog at the tree's soaring apex.

As the Cannonball steamed closer, a howling Butch still bounding on ahead, Jess glanced down at the track the loco was now rolling over, noting with hammering heart that the rails beneath had begun to rise from the rocky ground, borne by the first outlying elements of that insane steel support network. And up ahead, Jess could see quite clearly where that same track would soon be taking them. There was no doubt about it. None whatsoever.

"Okay, so, um, correct me if I'm wrong here, babe," Sally said, "but are we *really* just about to drive a train up a frickin tree?"

16

The Tree

As the Cannonball rolled on up the gentle incline, and the loco's front wheels finally attained a length of track fixed directly to the giant tree's lowermost bough, Jess found herself jerked out of her wordless wonder by another howl. Not Butch this time though. This howl arrived care of the cab's voice tube communication system and was recognizable instantly as Sissy, back there in the crew car with Miss Lacey, Dave, and Vera.

Several more howls followed the first, before over the top of them there came Miss Lacey's excited voice: "Ms. Flint, do you hear that? I think she remembers. I think she *actually* remembers."

Jess smiled. "Yup, hearing her loud and clear," she said into the voice tube horn.

Outside the cab windows, vast green leaves brushed by as the train, steaming onward, began to spiral its way around the giant tree, gaining height with every circuit. Ahead of them, Butch, clearly more at home up here than on the barren ground beneath, began to spend as much time swinging from vines and branches as he did galloping along on foot atop the boughs the track was fixed to. And all the while, he continued to shoot those regular glances back over his hairy shoulder, as if checking to see that the Cannonball (that *Sissy*) was still behind him.

Higher and higher the train climbed, the rusty and pitted track beneath it holding rock steady—a combination of the giant tree's natural density and the cunning design of the supporting steelwork, Jess presumed. As a feat of engineering, the whole thing almost defied logic. Defied *belief* even. Surely the tree's continued growth would pull the rails apart over time. Could the vast organism's natural rate of development really be that slow? And exactly how old *was* this track anyway? To Jess it looked positively *ancient*. As to why anyone would even want to run a railroad up a tree in the first place... So many many questions...

Jess's musings were interrupted by Sally beside her, the stoker now apparently the stoked:

"Sorry, babe," the gal said, "I just *gotta* see this from up top," with which she hauled herself through the cab's roof hatch to drop into the gunner's seat above.

A moment later, Sal's awe-tinged voice—and it took not a little to inspire awe in Sally 'Seen It All' Chu—emerged from the cab's voice tube: "Oh, my god, Jess, this is just *incredible!* You *gotta* come up here and see. It's like— WHOAH! STOP! PULL UP! NOW!"

Jess's heart leapt. "Sal? *Sal,* what is it?"

"I SAID STOP! NOW!" Sally yelled, and with a red rush of adrenalin, Jess shoved the throttle forward and lunged for the brake, slamming it fully closed in one.

At the Cannonball's current easy-does-it speed, the sudden deceleration was in no way risky, but a screech of brakes rang out nonetheless, and sparks fountained from the loco's locked drive wheels as the entire train ground to a juddering halt.

A beat later, Sally dropped in again through the roof hatch, motioned for Jess to follow, and then leapt from the cab, out onto the colossal bough atop which the train had come to a stop.

Clambering after Sally, Jess landed trackside by her frowning friend, and together the pair of them began to make their way forward along the broad bough, keeping carefully between the track's two rails and stepping over crossties as they went.

After only a dozen or so paces, they reached it—the hazard that an eagle-eyed Sally had spotted from the Cannonball's gun turret.

It was a section of broken track, an entire length of steel rail missing from one side.

Damn, but that had been close, Jess thought, trying not to imagine her beloved Cannonball crashing down through the branches below, to be smashed to scrap on the rocky ground at the foot of the tree.

For a moment or two more, Jess and Sally stood there pondering the gap in the rails while, on the other side of it, a somber Butch crouched in silence, still as a statue, staring at them with those oh-so-nearly-human eyes.

"We *could* just carry on on foot," Sal suggested. "Can't be that far now, surely."

Jess squinted into the impenetrable shadows beyond the foliage that surrounded them, then looked over again at Butch… to find him no longer as still and as silent as he had been just moments before. An attitude of animal alertness seemed now to have stiffened the creature's muscular frame, and he stood there fully upright, glancing all around and whining softly.

"Yeah, something tells me 'on foot' might be a real bad idea here," Jess said, turning once more to study the broken track before them. Fortunately, broken track was hardly an unusual hazard on the many poorly-maintained railroads of Mars's Free Zones, and no self-respecting train crew ever set forth into those regions without the requisite emergency gear and supplies. "Standard gauge, standard fixings," Jess said to Sally. "You wanna grab the needful?"

Returning a nod, Sal about-faced and set off again for the loco, while at the same time, disembarking from the crew car, Vera, Dave, and Miss Lacey began to approach, a wide-eyed Sissy tagging along behind them, resplendent still in Sally's 'Parisian one hundred percent silk'.

"Okay, just gonna say it," Dave shouted across to Jess as he drew nearer with the others, "so this'll be what they call a branch line."

"Get back inside the train," Jess said. "*Now.*"

"Oi!" Dave complained. "It weren't *that* bad."

"Inside," Jess said again. "I mean it. I think something might be—" but before she could finish there was a thud beside her, and suddenly there was Butch, right at Jess's shoulder, growling and moaning, baring his tusk-like canines, leaping about in agitation.

No, *more* than agitation.

Fear.

Vera's nervous tremolo only added to the escalating tension: "Jess? Jess, what is it? Why is he—" and before *she* could finish, there was *another* sound. Nothing so benign as a thud this time though. It was a shriek. A monstrous, gut-wrenching, animal shriek. It came from almost directly above, and as Jess's eyes shot to its source, she had to stifle a shriek of her own.

Because barreling towards her over a high branch, its monstrous jaws stretched wide, was a huge armored snake creature. Even bigger than the one they'd encountered in The Town With No Name, the shreksak hurtled straight at Jess and her friends like some kind of runaway train from hell, scimitar fangs dripping saliva, red eyes burning with bloodlust, demonic screams tearing at the air.

Jess opened her mouth to yell at the others, but once again found her words cut off, this time by a *second* shriek from an entirely *different* direction. And over the shoulders of the terrified group facing her, Jess saw *another* snake creature, this one racing towards them from the other end of the Cannonball.

At last, Jess's spiraling terror found its voice. "RUN!" she screamed.

17

Shreksak Attack

Butch was the first to react, bounding past Jess with a furious roar and heading straight for Sissy. A heartbeat later, the others took off too, Vera in the lead, Dave and Sally each grabbing one of Miss Lacey's arms and all but dragging the old lady along as the four humans plus two terrified creatures raced for the Cannonball.

Alone now by the length of broken track, and separated from the rest of the group by more than twenty meters, Jess launched herself after her fleeing friends, still unable to drag her eyes away from the blood-chilling sight of the second shreksak, speeding towards them from the rear of the train.

Oh god oh god oh god oh god, Jess's horrified mind babbled as she ran. *How can these things be so fast?* and already dreading what she might see, she risked a glance over her shoulder—

—only to have her heart leap with still more terror. Because the *first* shreksak—the one *behind* her—was closing in at a rate Jess could scarcely believe, shrieking its animal fury, fanged jaws agape. In seconds, those very same jaws would be snapping at Jess's pounding heels.

Up ahead, Jess saw Vera lurch past the far end of the coal tender and haul open the door of the sleeper car. A split-second later, while a terrified Vera stood holding the door for them, Dave, Sally, and Miss Lacey stumbled inside. Sissy and Butch followed instantly, then Vera herself, clambering up onto the carriage's step and turning Jess's way.

"Oh, god, Jess! Run! RUN!" Vera screamed from the open doorway.

But no. Not a chance. Jess could already see that she wouldn't make it to the sleeper car. Both the shreksak ahead of her and the one behind were now less than ten meters away, Jess caught directly between them. "Get inside! Shut the door!" she screamed to Vera, before taking the only action left that might yet save her life. Hanging a hard right, Jess threw herself into the loco's cab, scrambled across the footplate to the engine's alien-tech control panel—

—and pounded a fist into the button that activated the Cannonball's shields.

The button flashed once with an accompanying low beep, and then… silence.

Through a side window, as she lay panting in a corner of the cab, Jess could just make out the faint shimmer of the force-field that now surrounded the Cannonball and its rolling stock. Times like this, Jess didn't give a damn that the workings of the loco's alien-tech enhancements remained a mystery she'd barely begun to solve. Enough that those enhancements did their job. That the shields were up. Question was: did she get them up in *time?*

Heart still pounding, Jess crept on all fours to the open rear of the cab, peering around its beveled steel edge to see what the view outside might reveal—

—and with an ear-shattering crash, the shreksak exploded in through a forward window, fragments of glass raining down on Jess as the howling creature lunged straight at her.

•••

Gasping in terror, Vera stumbled on after the others down the corridor of the sleeper car. Up ahead, she saw Dave yank wide the door at the corridor's far end, shoulder open the heavy steel door of the adjoining crew car, then tumble through both with Sally, Miss Lacey, and the two creatures. An instant later, Vera followed, slamming the metal door closed behind her.

As Sissy and Butch stomped about, roaring their fury, Vera rushed with the others to the center of the crew car and peered out its single un-boarded up window, only to frown in surprise when she saw outside a faint but familiar rippling glow.

"Looks like Jess got the shields up," Sally said. "*Damn,* I shoulda thought of that. Okay then, so with a bit of luck, neither of those snake things will have gotten in. Maybe we'll be—"

A thunderous crash from above shook the entire carriage, and Vera's eyes shot upwards to the ceiling—

—just as the crew car's skylight came cascading down at her in a glittering torrent of glassy shards. The gaping jaws of a shreksak followed, and as what must have been a ton or more of armored snake-flesh surged through the smashed skylight, Vera threw herself to one side, the creature slamming into the crew car's floor almost dead center, in the exact spot Vera had just vacated.

But while her quick reaction undoubtedly saved her life, Vera saw right away that, for her at least, things had just gotten significantly worse. Because while *she,* in the terror of the moment, had dodged in one direction, *the others* had darted the opposite way, leaving the shreksak in the middle of the car, and Vera alone, separated from the rest of the group.

Isolate the weakest from the pack. That's what hunters did, Vera knew, and as its scaly head whipped her way, Vera was sure she saw the snake monster's eyes flash with animal exhilaration, before it reared up to the ceiling, hissed its reptilian fury, then came rocketing straight at her.

Even as the others screamed for her to run, Vera turned and fled, hauling open the end door she'd just come through, stumbling back out into the corridor of the sleeper car, and slamming both doors shut behind her—crew car's then sleeper's.

Through the tiny aligned windows of the two doors, Vera saw the pursuing shreksak smash hard into the crew car's heavy steel door, then reel back, shaking its monstrous head in a rage. Shrieking once more, the snake creature turned in place and began immediately to race back the way it had come, hurtling towards Sally and the others in the doorway at the opposite end of the crew car. Heart hammering, Vera watched the group there whirl in terror and then disappear through the exit, pulling the far door shut behind them.

"Oh my golly," Vera gasped, reaching out to steady herself against a wall panel just as—

—BANG!—the door at the other end of the sleeper corridor flew open, and Jess came diving through it, her face a crazed mask of fear.

"Jess!" Vera cried as her friend sprinted towards her. "One of those things got in!"

"*Two* of those things!" Jess yelled back, and even as Vera's innards lurched with yet *more* horror, she launched herself forward, she and Jess racing headlong at each other to collide in the middle of the passageway, where they shoved open a sleeping cabin, tumbled inside, and slammed shut the cabin door.

Crouched with Jess behind the flimsy door panel, Vera's stomach turned over yet again as she heard the crunch of splintering wood from the corridor outside. It came from the loco end of the train—the direction Jess had appeared from. The *other* shreksak, Vera realized, smashing its way through the end door of the timber-built sleeper wagon. A second later, Vera's fears were confirmed by a shocking rush of sound—a kind of creaking, scraping clatter that swept from left to right as the monster in the passageway outside slithered past the door Vera and Jess were hunkered behind. Eventually, a further jolting crash rocked the carriage—what could only be Jess's shreksak meeting the heavy *steel* door of the crew car at the corridor's other end.

Dead silence followed, and Vera turned her terror-wide eyes to Jess.

What now?

●●●

Barreling down the corridor of the VIP carriage, Sally came to a skidding stop outside the car's main cabin, thrust open the door, and threw herself inside. In a frenzied rush, Dave, Miss Lacey, Sissy, and Butch followed, tumbling in after Sally, who slammed the door behind them all and began to glance about for anything they could use to barricade the entrance.

Sally's heart sank instantly. Almost nothing of any significant size in the VIP cabin—in *any* of the passenger or crew cabins, for that matter—was freestanding, most of what was there bolted firmly to the carriage floor. Some chairs, a small wooden writing desk, and the mattresses and bedding were about all Sally could see to use. Not much, but dammit they would have to do.

As Sissy and Butch continued to stomp about and yowl their fury, Sally whirled on the others. "We need to keep that snake thing outta here," she barked, grabbing the nearest chair and jamming it under the door handle. After pausing just long enough to exchange mutual looks of terror, both Dave and Miss Lacey leapt into action and began to pile the rest of the compartment's scant freestanding furnishings against the cabin door...

●●●

Huddled with Vera in the cramped confines of the sleeping compartment, Jess pressed an ear to the door panel, listening…

Silence.

Was that thing still out there in the corridor? Waiting for Jess and Vera to give themselves away?

Because they certainly hadn't heard it go…

Motioning for Vera to stay quiet, Jess reached for the door handle, turned it, then edged open the cabin door as quietly as she could.

Beyond the doorframe was a solid wall of stationary snake flesh, pulsing gently.

With a start of shock, Vera jammed one hand over her mouth, and as she stumbled back a step, her left shoulder collided with a high shelf above the sleeping compartment's bunk.

What happened next seemed to Jess to play out in blood-freezing slo-mo:

On the shelf above the bunk, a stack of Sally's gramophone records shifted, wobbled for a moment on the very cliff edge of the shelf… and then fell. Jess could only watch in horror as almost the entire pile of records crashed to the floor, shattering the breathless silence in the sleeper cabin. Beside Jess, a second hand flew to Vera's mouth, failing this time to stifle the gal's whimper of terror. Jess cried out too, unable to stop herself.

But the snake creature didn't respond.

For several seconds more, Jess and Vera stood

there panting in fear, but the wall of snake flesh blocking the cabin doorway shifted not a centimeter in either direction.

Maybe hearing wasn't a shreksak's strong suit, Jess thought, her brain working still more furiously, trying to conjure a way out of this madness. Perhaps if they could—

—and then one final gramophone record fell from the shelf above the bunk, this one hitting the floor edge on, before bouncing twice and rolling its way across the width of the cabin floor—

—straight into the shreksak's pulsing hide.

Instantly, the pulsing ceased, and with heart-stopping suddenness the glistening wall of flesh began to reverse, scaly armored snake hide rushing back the way it had come, back towards the open doorway...

18

Sleeper Car of Horror

Slamming the door on the rushing blur of snake flesh, Jess whirled to Vera and grabbed her terrified friend by the shoulders. "Okay, here's the plan," she said, then rattled through her one half-baked and frankly all-but-suicidal idea.

Moments later, as the creature in the corridor outside began to batter against the flimsy wooden door, Vera, boosted by Jess, clambered out the window of the sleeping compartment and up onto the top of the carriage. As the English gal found her footing on the sleeper car's flat roof, Jess stuck her own head out the window, shot a glance right, then left… and gasped in shock when she saw the *other* shreksak slither from the skylight of the crew car behind. Facing away from Jess and Vera, the second snake monster paused momentarily on the crew car's roof, and for one horrifying second, Jess was sure the creature was going to turn and spot the exposed and helpless Vera. Clearly thinking the same, Vera froze where she stood, eyes wide with fear.

But the shreksak *didn't* turn. Instead, it slithered away over the roof of the crew car, heading towards the rear of the train, where, Jess prayed, Sally and the others were still hanging in there.

"Go!" Jess mouthed silently at Vera, and with a final terrified nod, the gal took off over the roof of the sleeper carriage, sprinting in the direction of the loco.

• • •

With a grunt of anger, Sally yanked the mattress from the VIP car's lower bunk and heaved it towards the rest of the furnishings now piled against the cabin door.

"Get the other one!" Sally yelled at Dave and Miss Lacey, who nodded and made a collective dive for the compartment's top bunk. As the pair hauled the second mattress from its high platform and dragged it to the door, Sissy and Butch continued to stomp and thrash, the cabin reverberating with their furious screeches.

"This is pointless," Dave shouted over the racket as he and Miss Lacey thrust the mattress onto the barricade. "No way is this gonna keep those things out!"

The guy was right, of course. As barricades went, Sally knew that what they'd built was pitiful. But hey, it was better than nothing, and if it bought them even a few seconds it might just—

With a heart-stopping shriek, the head of the shreksak came exploding in through the window behind, rocketing straight past Butch and Sissy and lunging for the group by the door.

Even Sally screamed.

•••

With her back to the open window of the sleeping compartment, Jess wrenched the cabin's fire extinguisher from the wall beside her and raised it to shoulder level, wielding the heavy steel cylinder club-like in both hands.

Opposite her, the cabin door continued to rattle and bang as the monster in the corridor outside rammed into the flimsy wooden paneling again and again, roaring its fury between every attack. In the tiny, one-bunk compartment, the sound was beyond deafening.

Then at last, in a crashing explosion of splinters and shattered hardware, the door burst inward, and Jess gasped as a blur of razor fangs and slitted red eyes came surging towards her.

With a roar of her own, she swung the fire extinguisher hard, landing just enough of a blow to send the startled shreksak into a momentary retreat.

"Vera! Please tell me you're there!" Jess bellowed into the voice tube horn by the cabin's bunk, and almost collapsed in relief when she heard Vera's voice come back:

"Yes, I'm in the cab! Should I—"

"DO IT!" Jess yelled. "DO IT NOW!"

From the voice tube there came a faint CLICK-HUM, and directing a glance over her shoulder through the open window, Jess saw the shield around the train wink out.

Now or never.

Lobbing the fire extinguisher at the monster in the doorway, Jess hoisted herself out through the window, dropped down over the car's exterior paneling—

—and that was when the whole plan went to hell. Because on the way down, Jess's left foot caught on some unforeseen protrusion, causing her to land badly. *Very* badly. A bolt of white-hot pain lanced through Jess's twisted ankle, and then blazed all the way up her lower leg as she clambered to her feet again on the massive tree bough. Clenching her jaw, Jess fought back the agony and stumbled away from the carriage, shooting a single terrified glance over her shoulder—

—and then instantly wishing she hadn't. Because behind her, the shreksak was already surging through the sleeper car window in pursuit, closer behind than Jess had planned for. *Much* closer behind.

Heart thudding like a jack-hammer, Jess staggered on four more steps, gritted her teeth, and then launched herself from the branch she was on, sailing over a yawning chasm of greenery to alight on the branch opposite. She landed better this time…

… at least until she tried to rise again and her injured ankle gave way beneath her, folding up all at once in another explosion of pain. Turning as she fell, Jess's back went slamming into the bough beneath, and when she looked up once more, her fear-fueled mind blotted out all but two things: the massive shrieking snake monster barreling straight at her, its back half still emerging from the carriage window; and Vera Middleton, watching all in open-mouthed disbelief from the rear of the loco. With a scream of horror, the English gal hauled herself back into the cab, vanishing from Jess's view.

But it was too late, Jess knew. *Way* too late. Because the creature was already—

And just as the oncoming shreksak was stretching its jaws wider still, as if to devour its helpless prey whole, Jess saw the air between her and the sleeper car ripple. "*YES!*" her adrenalin-stoked brain hollered as the Cannonball's shields re-engaged around the train—

—and sliced the charging shreksak neatly in two.

For another full second, the front half of the bisected snake monster sailed on through the air, before slamming into a branch several meters behind Jess, then plummeting into the darkness of the leafy abyss. At the same time, the creature's severed back half, tail end still squeezing through the carriage window, twitched, sagged, and then, with a last squirming spasm, finally slumped the rest of the way out of the sleeper car in a gush of spurting blood and spilling entrails.

•••

As the shreksak's hissing snakehead came at her for a third time, Sally dodged clear yet again, the creature's dagger-like fangs sinking into floorboards with a jarring crunch. Half the monster's scaly length had now made it through the window of the VIP car, and not for the first time since joining Jess and her crew, Sally regretted with a passion that they didn't 'do guns'. Cos how else were they supposed to *kill* this frickin thing?

Shaking carpet fragments and timber splinters from its teeth, the shreksak snorted in rage, drew back several meters, and then whirled on Dave, lunging for the fella at blinding speed. With a yell of fright, Dave threw himself to one side, and the creature's monstrous jaws snapped shut just millimeters shy of the guy's fleeing ass.

In the opposite corner of the cabin, Sissy and Butch howled and stomped, frenzied and furious, while over by the barricaded door, Miss Lacey grabbed an item from the top of their feeble blockade and hurled it at the writhing, hissing snake monster.

Yeah, like that's *gonna help,* Sally thought, before, sure enough, the flimsy wooden chair simply bounced off the shreksak's armored hide and went clattering across the floor.

But then, just as the creature was turning its nightmarish gaze on Miss Lacey, Sally spotted an opening and launched herself forward, landing a full-power roundhouse kick right in the monster's slitted red eye. She felt her boot-heel sink into something pulpy and gelatinous, and with a howl of pain the creature reared back, shaking its massive head. A second later, howling still, the shreksak hauled itself back out through the carriage window to vanish into the greenery beyond.

Not that the heart-stopping stuff was over quite yet though, a resounding CRASH from behind setting Sally and the others whirling in shock to find—

—Jess and Vera, standing there in the open doorway of the car, amidst the remains of the useless barricade.

Sally sagged in relief. "*Damn it,* girl," she said to Jess, "please don't—"

She never finished the sentence. Because that was when the shreksak came surging in again through the window and, before any of them could so much as gasp, snatched a petrified Dave where he stood. With one casual toss of its reptilian head, the creature sent the screaming guy tumbling down its gaping, fleshy gullet, then an instant later, the shreksak's monstrous jaws slammed shut, and Dave Hart was gone.

19

End of the Line

How long they all stood there, paralyzed by the sheer horror of it, Vera never knew. Probably only seconds, but to her it felt like an eternity.

And in the end, it wasn't even one of the humans who finally broke that tableaux of terror.

It was Sissy.

With a roar of rage that quite literally shook the walls of the VIP cabin, the creature in Sally's ballgown bounded forward, leapt onto the back of the shreksak's head, and launched into her counterattack: punching, clawing, biting, wrenching—a tornado of terrifying violence that surely even the snake monster's armored hide would fail to survive.

But survive it did, the shreksak howling in ferocious defiance as it tried to throw Sissy off, battering her silk-clad form against ceiling, walls, floor. All around, glass shattered, timber splintered, and metalwork crumpled, but still Sissy clung on, her rage undiminished, her room-shaking cries louder than ever.

Then all at once, Butch was there too, springing forward with a roar of his own to grab one side of the snake monster's tossing head. As Vera and the others continued to watch helplessly—right now, it was all *they* could do to avoid being crushed by the shreksak's thrashing bulk—Sissy and Butch wrestled the creature's head to the floor, where, with one further heave, Butch twisted the monstrous reptile so that a length of its unarmored neck and underbelly lay exposed.

That was when the full horror of the situation finally came crashing in on Vera, because beneath the snake creature's lower jaw, but above its main muscled body area, there was a massive bulge. A massive *moving* bulge. *Dave,* Vera realized, her stomach turning over in horror.

A split-second later, Sissy dropped to the floor, raised her deadly claws, and then swung them hard at the shreksak's exposed neck, just below the squirming bulge that was Dave. With almost no sound at all, Sissy's razor talons tore straight through the snake monster's unarmored throat, trailing ribbons of flesh and skin as they emerged on the far side.

Roaring in pain, and with a shrieking Butch still clinging tight to its head, the shreksak bucked and heaved, blood and mucous gushing from its gaping neck wound in a greasy, gleaming torrent. Then, at last, with a gurgling cry of horror, Dave came tumbling from the ragged gash in the shreksak's throat to flop groaning onto the carriage floor. A second after that, the defeated snake monster gave one final whimper, one terminal twitch, and lay still.

In a glistening pool of the creature's bodily fluids, Dave, unharmed as far as Vera could see, began to drag himself upright, but had barely made it onto his elbows when, with a howl of emotion, Sissy fell to her knees beside the lad, scooped him into her hairy arms, and began to smother him with kisses, keening loudly.

Next to the entwined pair, a silent but panting Butch stood looking on, and it wasn't long before Sissy turned to the male creature, appeared to consider matters for a beat, then reached out to pull him into a huddle with her and Dave, smothering *Butch* with kisses now too.

And through it all—through every last bizarre but heart-lifting moment—neither Vera, Jess, nor Miss Lacey could find a single word to say.

Sally, of course, was another matter, and after several more seconds of watching Sissy plant kiss after kiss upon both Dave *and* a clearly delighted Butch, the smiling Ms. Chu finally opened her mouth to offer comment.

Dave, though, was having none of it and raised a warning forefinger. "Swear to god, Sal," he said, "I hear the word *three-way* come outta your gob, you are making your *own* damn coffee from now on."

●●●

As the Cannonball Express maintained its slow, cautious spiral up the giant tree, Butch once again leading the way, soft saxes and lilting strings permeated the air of the crew car, drifting over to Vera from the gramophone in the corner. Barely half an hour on from the horror of the shreksak attack, the soothing effect of the music was, Vera thought, rather welcome right now. *Highly* welcome in fact. And clearly she was not the only one to think so—at the other end of the carriage, keeping perfect time with the music, Sissy and Dave continued the slow, romantic foxtrot they'd been engaged in for the last several minutes, Sissy's cheek resting gently on her partner's compliant shoulder. With her borrowed ballgown now ragged and bloody, and those near-human eyes of hers fixed intently upon the boy in her arms, the picture presented was, to Vera at least, as unexpectedly touching almost as it was bizarre, prompting Vera to wonder if a creature such as Sissy could actually feel something as supposedly sophisticated as love. Had she been asked such a question right at this very moment, Vera would surely have been forced to say yes. *Absolutely* yes.

As for Sissy's unlikely dance partner? Well... the expression on *his* face was, as might be imagined, significantly more complex, if not entirely unreadable.

"Dave, are you *sure* you're all right?" Vera asked.

"I'm fine, Vera," the boy replied. "Honestly, I am. Besides, after what she done, lady wants a dance, lady gets a dance."

Which, of course, was all but impossible to argue with.

"And hey, guess what?" Dave continued, brightening a little. "Think I'm *actually* improving. I ain't even stood on her feet for—"

Sissy gave a sudden yelp, pulling her crushed toes out from beneath Dave's size tens then whacking the lad gently on the side of his head.

"Yeah, well, getting there, ain't I?" Dave said with a lopsided grin.

Next to Vera, Miss Lacey, who up until now had sat in pensive silence, intent once more upon her knitting, looked over at the dancing couple, her brow host to a frown of motherly concern that seemed of late to be a near permanent fixture there. "You do know this will just make it even harder for her," the old lady said to Dave. "When we eventually have to…"

"I know," Dave said, turning his partner neatly at the end of the aisle to head back the way they'd come. *Nicely done,* Vera thought in passing. 'Getting there' the boy actually *was.*

"I'll think of something, I promise," Dave continued, and was just opening his mouth to say more when the car gave a sudden but gentle jerk, causing Dave and Sissy to stumble mid-step.

"Hey, I think we're stopping," Vera said, and sure enough, outside the carriage window, the horizontal flow of greenery began to slow. Seconds later, it halted completely, and a moment after that, Jess's voice emerged from the horn of the crew car's voice tube:

"Okay, folks, looks like this is it. End of the line."

● ● ●

Climbing down from the Cannonball's cab, Jess hopped off the lowermost rung of the rear access ladder to land trackside by a silent Butch and a wide-eyed Sally.

"What the frickin hell *is* this place?" Sal said, her voice uncharacteristically hushed.

146

What the frickin hell indeed…

As Vera and the others disembarked from the crew car behind and began to approach, Jess let her eyes rove over what the Cannonball Express stood parked beside—the mysterious building they'd seen at the top of the tree.

Single story and badly dilapidated, the structure—some kind of ancient pre-fab by the looks of it—was a lot bigger than it had appeared from below, with a sizeable rail platform running the length of its ruined façade, and what had to be centuries worth of botany—vines and creepers as well as branches of the tree itself—weaving its way through the crumbling remains of the building's walls. Overall, the construction looked manmade to Jess, rather than alien, a suspicion that was all but confirmed a moment later when she pulled aside some climbing weeds from a badly weathered sign above a battered door:

"…CIENCE STATIO…08758", the surviving, only just legible part of the sign read.

As to the actual *age* of the building though, that was considerably *less* clear to Jess. Two hundred years maybe? Three? Perhaps even—

But before she could consider the question further, a cacophony of ear-splitting animal shrieks rang out from behind, and even as Jess whirled in shock with the others, she felt the timber platform beneath her shudder as a dozen or more howling creatures dropped from the greenery above, rose up onto their clawed feet, and launched themselves at the five terrified humans.

20

The Tribe

That the howling creatures thundering towards Jess and her friends were of the same species as Sissy and Butch, there could be no doubt—the tribe's silver-gray fur and simian features told all there. Unfortunately, what was also beyond doubt was that, same species or not, these animals were ready to tear the five human interlopers to ragged and bloody pieces.

Adrenalin surging, Jess whirled, ready to bolt with the others for the Cannonball, but before she—before *any* of them—took even one step, Butch reared up and darted forward, roaring back in defiance of the attacking creatures—

—who immediately broke off their howling and stopped dead in their tracks.

A protracted and breathless silence followed, during which Jess's heart hammered against her ribcage, her muscles as tense as tempered steel.

Eventually, one of the new creatures—an elderly female, by the looks of it—broke away from the rest of the tribe and loped up to Butch, pausing in front of the male creature for a moment, before going on to sniff at him for several long seconds.

What happened next took them all by complete surprise.

Withdrawing from Butch just long enough to make the most glancing of eye contact, the elderly female threw both arms around the male animal, hugging him hard. And yet again, as with Sissy on previous occasions—Butch too, come to that—Jess couldn't help but be struck by how *human* the she-creature's actions looked; so filled with a clear and unambiguous emotional intelligence.

But then the mood hair-pinned for a second time, the elderly female's eyes darting once more to Jess and co, a dangerous growl rumbling in the creature's throat.

Again though, Butch intervened, bounding back to the group by the Cannonball and draping arms around both Sissy and Dave, while at the same time emitting an extended series of grunts and growls—expressive and complex and, to Jess at least, more than suggestive of actual language.

The elderly female waited until Butch had finished his guttural oration, after which, while clearly still wary, she lurched up to Jess and her friends and ran her intense animal gaze over the entire group. When she came at last to Sissy, huddled in fear behind Miss Lacey's skirts, the old she-creature paused, cocking a puzzled head at the young female's torn and bloody ballgown. Then, just as she had done with Butch, the elderly female raised her twitching muzzle to sniff at Sissy herself. During the tense and curiously intimate moment, a trembling Sissy clung whimpering to Miss Lacey, but as it turned out, Sissy's ordeal was short-lived, because almost immediately, the old she-creature drew back again, her eyes widening in what, to Jess, looked a whole lot like astonishment.

An instant later, and with her every darting movement suggesting some kind of enormous excitement, the elderly female was off once more, bounding for an open doorway nearby. There, she paused briefly in the doorframe to yowl over her shoulder at Jess and the gang, then promptly vanished through the exit in a flash of silver-gray fur.

For another long moment, Jess and the others stood there exchanging looks of deepest uncertainty. If nothing else, Jess had at least expected the rest of the tribe to follow the elderly female through the door. But they hadn't. The remaining creatures continued simply to crouch there in complete silence, their dark eyes fixed intently upon Jess and the gang.

"Okay then," Jess said eventually. "So… I guess we're… invited *in?*"

Taking her crew's silence for assent, Jess led off, the group making their way across the rail platform and past that silent gauntlet of unnerving animal scrutiny, before filing through the doorway the old she-creature had disappeared into.

With not the slightest idea of what might lie beyond it, Jess stepped over the threshold to find herself in a vast, open-plan, interior space, the encroaching greenery here as evident as it had been on the building's crumbling exterior. Row after row of battered stainless steel workbenches, along with walls sporting the vestiges of cupboards and shelving, suggested to Jess some kind of ancient laboratory, while underfoot (and bolstering Jess's 'laboratory' conjecture) were the broken and crushed remains of assorted technical equipment, still visible beneath the dense carpet of creepers and weeds. More creatures lurked here too, squatting in silence on the steel benches or perched atop surviving cupboards.

As she glanced about, Jess noted also that the lab, if such it had indeed been, was almost completely missing its roof, a broad swathe of blue sky visible above; while over at the farthest end of the huge space, the entire back wall was gone too, the floor there ending in what looked to be a cliff edge plummet.

"Anyone see where Ms. Huggy went?" Jess asked the others.

Sally shook her head. "Not me," she said. "Looked like a lady on a mission though, don't you think? Maybe she's—"

Sal never finished, cut off mid-sentence as a heart-stopping BOOM! rocked the ancient laboratory, the floor beneath Jess's feet trembling in response. Trembling like the rail platform had done with the arrival of the tribe only minutes before.

Yes, *exactly* like that.

Only bigger.

Much bigger.

"Whoah!" Dave blurted. "What the hell was—"

And once again—BOOM!—the impact sending dust clouds rising from the lab floor.

Then BOOM-BOOM-BOOM-BOOM, for all the world like giant footsteps heading their way.

"Ah…" Miss Lacey said, the tone of that lone monosyllable suggestive to Jess of a woman who *knew* what the frickin hell might be going on here.

Clearly catching the same tone, Sally whirled

on the old lady. "*Ah...?* What do you mean *Ah...?* Cos me? Not a huge fan of sentences beginning with *Ah...*"

But Miss Lacey didn't answer, and as the lab continued to shake with those resounding sub-bass impacts, the creatures poised all around began to reciprocate with a kind of hushed, communal murmur—expressions, Jess was almost certain, of intense anticipation, fear, *awe* even.

BOOM-BOOM-BOOM-BOOM!

"Oh, god," Dave whimpered, "what *is* that?"

Then BOOM!—the elderly female reappeared all at once in a huge open doorway—

—before—BOOM!—darting aside again, as if to clear the way.

And with a final, room-rattling KA-BOOM! it thrust its way into the lab—a towering, silver-maned colossus of a creature, once again the same species as Sissy but easily seven times her size. Titanic muscles rippling beneath its gleaming fur, flesh-tearing canines dripping saliva, the hulking behemoth stomped forward into the center of the vast space, then reared up to its full terrifying height, roaring at the sky above and beating its gargantuan chest with a sound like thunder.

21

Momma

The immense creature, a heart-stopping vision of primal power and majestic ferocity, rooted Jess—rooted *all* of them—to the spot, its deafening roar and thunderous chest-beating an apocalyptic assault on the senses.

"Holy mother of…" Sally began, before lapsing into a choked silence when the monster abruptly broke off its display and, with a last floor-shaking BOOM!, deposited itself in the center of the lab. Thereafter, the massive animal fell into a silence of its own and continued simply to sit there, peering down at Jess, her crew, Miss Lacey…

… and Sissy, who, whining in terror, ducked

behind Miss Lacey, cowering into the old woman's voluminous skirts.

"Hmmmm," Miss Lacey said. "Yes, I think *mother* may well be the appropriate term here…"

Jess frowned. *Mother?* That the huge creature was a mature female, there could be no doubt, but something in Miss Lacey's soft, marveling tone had seemed to Jess to imply a more *specific* meaning. Almost as if…

And even as that meaning finally clicked in Jess's boggling mind, the colossal she-beast cocked her head at Sissy, issued a gentle, rumbling moan, then opened her mighty arms.

The simple message could not have been clearer: *Come to Momma.*

If, by then, Jess had still harbored doubts that, somehow or other, this was indeed Sissy's biological mother they were dealing with, those doubts vanished completely when, finally, Jess registered 'Momma's' long, flowing mane—a thick and luxuriant fall of silver through which there ran a single streak of darkest black flecked with purest white.

Exactly like the streak that ran through Sissy's mane.

"But… but… her *size*," Jess said to Miss Lacey. "She's like… like an entirely different *species*."

The old lady shrugged. "Don't ask me to explain the biology here, Ms. Flint, but rumor has *always* held that some kind of grand matriarch leads these animals, even if, as far as I'm aware, no one has ever seen her in the flesh."

"So why is she showing herself *now?*"

Miss Lacey looked thoughtful. "At a guess, I'm thinking perhaps our Sissy may be even *more* important than we realized."

Jess frowned, eyeing once again the distinctive black streak in Momma's adult mane, then the version in miniature that Sissy sported. In all but size, the markings were identical, while more telling still was the fact that none of the other creatures seemed to possess such a mark. The implication was clear, and a smiling Miss Lacey eventually voiced it for them all:

"Perhaps our Sissy is even a potential matriarch herself."

"Hot *damn,*" Sally murmured, shaking her head in wonder. "Gal's a frickin *princess!*"

Once more, Momma yowled softly at Sissy, her outspread arms widening, beckoning, *urging* the trembling creature to come to her.

Again though, Sissy recoiled in fear, shrinking into Miss Lacey and burying herself ever more deeply in the old lady's skirts.

As for Miss Lacey herself, Jess could now see waves of deep emotion roiling beneath the woman's pale and exhausted features—waves that threatened any second to spill over in tears.

But then, after drawing in several deep breaths, Miss Lacey seemed to stand a little straighter, and gulping back her evident emotions, she nodded to the cowering Sissy, stroking the creature's hair with an infinite motherly tenderness, before gently ushering her in Momma's direction.

And this time, something seemed finally to get through to the terrified creature in the torn and bloody ballgown. Though clearly still uneasy, Sissy gave out a quiet moan, almost to herself, then began at last to shuffle her way towards the huge she-beast.

In response, Momma yowled again, the gigantic creature opening her arms wider still as her long lost daughter edged ever closer.

Step by tentative step, a nervous Sissy closed the distance between herself and Momma, the towering matriarch keening softly, low-toned rumbles of the gentlest encouragement, until eventually—

The roar of an engine ripped through the air, tearing the moment apart.

Jess cried out in shock, her heart vaulting in her chest as a two-seater biplane rocketed up and over the treetop building, vanishing again beyond a ridge of higher foliage.

What the hell?

Then, before Jess's lurching heart had even begun to settle, the plane came hurtling back over them in the opposite direction, the craft's vivid paintwork unmistakable this time round:

Petrovna's Famous Carnival of Mars.

An ear-splitting roar shook the treetop lab—Momma, rising to her full height and screaming her rage at the biplane as it started to bank, the aerial maneuver surely signaling another pass to come. Following Momma's lead, the rest of the tribe rose too, pounding their chests and howling at the aircraft, which, sure enough, began to head their way for a third time.

Jess shot Sally a wild look, and a beat later, the pair of them took off, racing for the opposite side of the lab, where the missing back wall might allow them to see out and assess the situation. Slamming to a stop at the cliff edge plummet where the floor ended, Jess glanced at the ground far below… and felt her stomach turn over as her very worst fears were confirmed.

Parked at the foot of the giant tree was the *Carnival of Mars* show train.

By Jess's shoulder, Sally spat out a vicious curse and punched a nearby branch. "I *knew* this was going too well. *Dammit!*"

Heartrate skyrocketing, Jess whirled to look back at the others by the lab's entrance, but before she could take even a single step to rejoin them, the attacking biplane completed its third thunderous pass.

And this time, it came bearing gifts.

Something came streaking from the aircraft's underside.

Two somethings.

Missiles, their dark contrails uncoiling behind them, black threads of doom in the blue sky.

"Everyone down!" Jess shouted even as the projectiles slammed into the floor of the lab.

But an explosion never came. Instead, the missiles began to spew out vast volumes of green smoke, and almost immediately, Jess felt the dense, billowing fumes catch at her throat.

She started to cough.

Beside her, Sally did too.

"Breathers!" Jess shouted, she and Sal launching themselves for the other side of the lab again—for the door they'd entered through. "There's breathers in the Cannonball! If we can just—" but an excruciating throat spasm stole the rest of her words, and even as she hacked out another cough, Jess felt the first waves of dizziness wash through her. Shaking her head to dispel the encroaching black, she staggered on, her eyes trained dead ahead on the door back to the Cannonball. But already that door was vanishing from Jess's view—lost behind a wall of billowing green fumes.

And then another two missiles came slamming

in, spewing yet more of the acrid green smoke.

Up ahead, Jess saw Vera stumble and collapse. Dave followed almost immediately, then a second later, Sally went down too, toppling mid-stride and slumping unconscious to the floor.

Finally, Jess herself flopped to the ground, waves of an ever deeper darkness crashing over her, sinking *into* her. And even as the black was obliterating the scant remains of her awareness, Jess registered one last horror—something that cut straight to her pounding heart and filled her with soul-crushing despair. Because it wasn't just the *humans* the gas was sedating. All around Jess, the *creatures* were beginning to sway and stagger too. The entire tribe. Every last one of them.

Even Momma.

• • •

Lounging against the cab of the show train's loco, Levi Zabulon Slinger took a long, lazy drag on the thin black cheroot that poked from between his lips and watched the biplane make its fourth pass over the ruined building atop the giant tree.

Beside him, Zora took a similar drag of her own from the massive hand-rolled stogie currently stuffed into her stony face, and as the distant airplane's final two gas missiles hit their mark, a tiny smile of satisfaction tweaked the corners of the woman's mouth.

On the verge of offering pithy comment at this, Slinger had barely opened his mouth to do so when, all of a sudden, something drew his attention back to the tree.

It was a sound.

A kind of heavy, resonating THUD.

Along with it, several branches at the very top of the tree shook visibly. Then, half a second later, more thuds followed—a whole series of them in fact—deep, pounding impacts that echoed off the crater's towering walls while, at the same time, still more of the tree's outer branches shuddered. Slinger watched the ongoing phenomenon with profound fascination, tracing with ease the movement of the disturbed foliage in an almost dead straight line—one heading inexorably downwards.

Yup. No question about it.

Something was falling from the tree.

Something *big*.

Almost a full thirty seconds later, the something in question finally slammed into rocky ground not ten meters from where Slinger and Zora stood, and as it did, the collective gasp from the carnival's goggle-eyed personnel—assembled in a variety of groups farther down the train—was loud, long, and, Slinger would be forced to admit, *entirely* merited.

For several seconds more, neither Slinger nor

Zora said a word—just turned open-mouthed to each other and then strolled forward in mute astonishment until they stood at the foot of the fallen object.

The *literal* foot—five-toed, silver-furred, and at least seven times the size of the ones on the creature they had actually come here for.

"Well then, Zabulon," Zora said at last, her hint-of-a-smile blooming almost to a fully-fledged grin as her gaze ran the length of the colossal, unmoving creature the giant foot was attached to, "Sissy or no Sissy, if *this* thing is still alive, you may just have earned yourself a generous bonus."

22

Full Throttle

A voice emerged from the darkness:

"Jess? Jess, you with me, babe?"

Then a face—*Sally's* face—blurring slowly into view.

"There's our gal," Sally said, crouched frowning over Jess while the others—Dave, Vera, Miss Lacey—lurked in a background still materializing from the haze. "You okay, hon?"

Jess squeezed her eyes shut and then opened them again, trying to clear the lingering befuddlement. "What… where…?" she finally managed, followed by, "Oh, god, my head," as blinding pain came rolling up in great, rusty,

164

overfilled trucks. Breathing through the agony, Jess glanced about her, noting even as she was fighting off the disorientation that she appeared to be outside, lying on some kind of vine-covered ground somewhere…

No, wait…

Not ground.

Floor.

The treetop lab.

And then it all came flooding back. The tribe, Momma, the attacking biplane.

Hauling herself onto her elbows, Jess shook off the last of her confusion, and as she scanned the room she lay sprawled in, her heart sank like lead. "Where are they? Where are the creatures? Sissy… The big one… Where's—"

"She *took* them." It was Miss Lacey who spoke, her voice at once choked with anguish and hoarse with fury. "Took Sissy. Took them *all*. The whole *tribe.*"

"We don't *know* that," Sally said. "Not for sure. I was the first to come round, and by that time they were already gone. All of them."

Dave took a step forward, the torment contorting his face easily a match for Miss Lacey's. "Sure or not, we gotta go after them. We *gotta,* Jess! It's *Sissy!*" His voice almost broke when he said the creature's name, and Vera moved in to lay a hand on the guy's shaking shoulder.

Still sprawled on the vine-covered floor, propped half-upright on her elbows, Jess looked again to Sally, whose frown grew deeper as she spoke once more:

"They got maybe a half hour's head start, but if they *do* have Sissy, going after them might well be our best shot at getting her back." Sal's frown deepened further still as she added, "Maybe our *only* shot," and reaching down, she offered Jess a hand.

Grabbing Sally's wrist, Jess hauled herself to her feet and then turned to the others. "Okay," she said, her heart racing, her muscles bowstring taught, "so what are we waiting for? Let's go!"

• • •

Squeezed into the observation turret atop Zora's personal carriage, Slinger peered out through the rear viewport at the bleak terrain of northern Mars, receding from the hurtling show train in a dusty red blur. Still no sign of the Flint gal's loco in pursuit, Slinger was relieved to note, although in his opinion, this was still far from a done deal. Previous experience had taught Slinger to exercise caution when dealing with Ms. Jessica Flint and her crew. *Extreme* caution. So nope, not until he, Zora, and their new acquisition were out of the Free Zones and back to relative civilization could they be confident in chalking this one up as a win.

On the subject of which 'acquisition', there, of course, was another potential problem they would do well to keep on top of. From his high vantage point in the carriage's observation turret, Slinger could see the huge she-beast chained to a flatbed at the very end of the show train, and while their colossal captive had survived her tumble from the tree largely unscathed—a result, Slinger imagined, of her incredibly solid build, as well as the numerous branches that had broken her fall on the way down—she was not, it would be fair to say, in a happy place. More concerning still, from the way the creature was twisting and writhing in her chains—starting to roar now too—it was clear that the tranquilizers Zora was using to keep the thing docile were starting to wear off. Again.

Slinger needn't have worried though. Even as he stepped down from the turret to inform Zora of the situation, he saw that she was already across it. Lounging on a plush, upholstered chaise in the red and gold opulence of her private cabin, the woman barked into a voice tube, "Think our gal might be getting a little antsy back there, Mack. I swear they can hear the damn critter in New Motown. Another hundred mils oughtta settle her. See to it, will ya?"

"Will do," came the response on the voice tube, quick and fearful—the way most people with a healthy survival instinct responded to Her

Imperial Majesty Zora Petrovna.

Satisfied for now, Slinger turned once again to step back up into the observation turret, but just as he was reaching for the hand rail, Zora's irritated tones stopped him short:

"Zab, for crying out loud, would you just *relax*. They are *not* gonna catch us, okay? Hell, I doubt any of 'em are even awake yet."

Slinger sighed and shook his head in frustration. "Okay, look, *you* do not *know* this crew, Zora. That loco of theirs? It's fast. *Real* fast. If anyone could—"

But before Slinger could finish, an unexpected sound cut through the rhythmic rumble of the show train's wheels. Protracted and piercing, it was a sound anyone who'd ever ridden the railroads of Mars could identify with ease—the shrill, piping blast of a steam-whistle.

Eyes widening, Slinger launched himself back up the observation turret's steps to glare again out the rear viewport.

"God *dang* it," he spat, as behind them on the single track railroad, surely not even a kilometer away, Slinger's very worst fear emerged from around a broad bend, thundering through swirling clouds of red dust and then hurtling into full view.

It was another loco.

But not just *any* loco. Of course not.

Its dazzling red livery and gleaming brasswork

glinting in the low evening sun, somehow the Cannonball Express had once again defied the odds.

And worse yet, the blasted thing was closing in. Closing in *fast*.

23

Showdown

In the cab of the Cannonball, Jess opened up the throttle further still, her beloved locomotive surging with yet more acceleration, the ear-splitting shriek of its steam-whistle seeming to vent the fury of everyone present—Jess, Vera, Dave, Miss Lacey. Framed in the cab's side windows, the rocky landscape of Mars flew past, while in the forward ones, the train they were chasing down the single track drifted in and out of view, a flickering target on the far side of its own dust storm wake.

Squinting ahead through the churning red clouds, Jess nodded. "Yup, that's Momma all right," she said, confirming what Vera had only just alerted them to—the huge she-beast, chained to a flatbed at the very rear of the train they were pursuing. None too pleased about it either, if the creature's struggles were any indication. "And if these scumbags have got *Momma,* chances are they've got Sissy and the rest of the tribe too."

Next to Jess, Dave released the chain for the steam-whistle, the high piercing howl of it shutting off instantly. "They ain't slowing," he said, glowering at the train in front.

"Never expected them to," Jess replied, "but hey, one warning is all they get," and wrenching a lever below the Cannonball's throttle, Jess both heard and *felt* a deep resonant clank, followed by the grinding thrum of the mechanism she'd just activated—the mechanism that drew aside two steel panels at the very front of the Cannonball and extended the loco's hidden forward coupling. Seconds later, a concluding clunk told Jess that the coupling was now in position and ready for action—

—at which point, damned if Lady Luck didn't cut them an unexpected but highly welcome break. Because even as Jess was considering the wisdom of a further speed increase, the track ahead of the two trains suddenly straightened out all the way to the horizon.

"Well okay then," Jess said to the others, "so

I'm thinking maybe time you all found yourselves something sturdy to hold onto," and warning duly dispensed, she slammed the heel of her hand into a button near the top of the Cannonball's alien-tech control panel.

Engine roaring like a monster uncaged, the loco gave a single, neck-jolting lurch and then surged forward with impossible acceleration, Vera, Dave, and Miss Lacey barely managing to grab that 'something sturdy' in time to stop themselves being rammed into the safety rail that ran across the cab's open back.

All around them, the Cannonball clanked and shrieked and rattled and banged, shaking like it might fall apart any moment, and Jess, not for the first time upon activating this particular 'alien enhancement', found herself offering up a prayer to Warwick Davis, the movie actor from ages past who had somehow ended up their own personal Saint Christopher. To the fella's smiling face, watching over them from a framed photo above the throttle, Jess mouthed a silent, *Don't let us down, Mr. D.*, then to the Cannonball herself, *Hold together, baby. You hear me? Just hold together.*

And hold together she did, still in one glorious piece when, fewer than ten seconds later, they finally sped into the dusty wake of the train ahead—

—whereupon, wouldn't ya just know it, Lady

Luck, true to her fickle form, promptly grabbed her coat and left the party.

Because that was when, through a break in the swirling clouds of red ahead, Jess saw a dark figure emerge from the window of a carriage halfway down the train they were chasing.

A head appeared first.

Then an arm.

Then another arm.

And another.

And in the fists that terminated each of those arms, three gleaming silver revolvers.

Even as Jess cried out to warn the others, Slinger loosed a thunderous volley of shots that slammed into the glass of the Cannonball's forward windows. On instinct alone, Jess ducked for cover, although she needn't have—the windows' toughened glass panels held, thank god, Slinger's bullets ricocheting off them into the rocky landscape beyond.

Jaw clenching, Jess hauled back harder still on the Cannonball's throttle and felt yet another surge of acceleration—

—while up ahead, beyond the show train's swirling dust cloud wake, the coupling on the rear of the flatbed wagon—the wagon Momma was chained to—moved in and out of view, surely only thirty meters away... make that twenty... now just ten...

... and then, at last, there came a bone-rattling jolt as, at the front of the loco, the Cannonball's forward coupling clanged into the corresponding coupling on the rear of the show train's flatbed.

Spinning again to the loco's control console, Jess wrenched yet another lever—the one that remotely lowered the forward coupling's locking pin—and then whirled on Dave beside her. By this time, words were redundant. A dip of Jess's chin communicated all, and returning a determined nod of his own, Dave hauled the loco's brake lever into its full-closed position.

Instantly, the ear-shredding screech of metal on metal drowned out every other sound in the cab, sparks from the Cannonball's locked drive wheels cascading past the side windows as the two trains, now essentially one, careered onwards. For several terrifying seconds, Jess was sure that, locked drive wheels or no locked drive wheels, the dead weight of the Cannonball wouldn't in the end be enough to stop the speeding show train—that they would all of them just be hauled the rest of the way back to civilization, there to be arrested en masse and thrown into some godforsaken Martian prison for the remainder of their pitiful lives.

But then Jess felt the train—the *two* trains— begin to slow; heard that shriek of metal on metal start to diminish. In the cab windows, the twin cascades of sparks on either side fell away—

—until at last, in a storm of flames and steam and dense black smoke, the two coupled trains ground to a jolting, juddering halt.

Even as the dust and smoke were still clearing from around the Cannonball, Jess leapt down from the cab, landed trackside—

—and immediately had to doubletake her surroundings. Because directly opposite the stretch of railroad upon which the two trains had come to a stop was a sight Jess had sincerely hoped never to have to look at again.

The Town With No Name.

In the settlement's filthy square, several of its inhabitants stood there agog, staring across at the two smoking locos, while in doors and windows all around, further mystified faces were already beginning to appear.

"Jess! Here!"

Spinning at Dave's call, Jess was just in time to see the guy toss something to her from the open rear of the Cannonball. The *something*—a two-stroke-fueled, hand-held angle grinder, ideal for cutting through thick steel chains—was one of a pair of such tools Jess kept aboard the loco, the second of that pair now slung over Dave's shoulder as he hopped down from the footplate to join Jess trackside. Vera and Miss Lacey were right behind the fella.

Through the still settling dust, the four of them raced together for the show train's rearmost wagon, on whose grimy steel flatbed a distressed Momma continued to roar and struggle, multiple lacerations—raw and bloody—visible where the rusting chains had cut into her.

Jess spun to Vera and Miss Lacey. "Go! Find Sissy and the others!" she ordered, before hauling the starting cord on her grinder. Dave followed suit, the two power tools springing to simultaneous life, and as Vera and Miss Lacey turned to go, Jess and Dave lowered the spinning blades of their grinders towards the chains holding Momma to the wagon.

But before either tool could begin its work:

"Jess, look out!"

It was Vera's voice, sharp with fear, and Jess looked up in time to see Slinger, all six of his weapons drawn, leap clear of the carriage he'd launched his previous assault from. Eyes shadowed beneath his jet black Stetson, the multi-armed gunslinger began to stalk their way.

"Oh, god, Jess, what do we do?" Vera babbled. "What do we—"

But then another voice. Low, dangerous, half-purr-half-snarl:

"S 'okay, gang. I got this."

And there she was.

Sally 'dammit-but-ya-gotta-love-that-gal' Chu.

All suited up in her steam-loader, glowering across at Slinger like he'd just borrowed her eyeliner without asking.

And *nobody* borrowed Sally's eyeliner without asking.

24

Round One

In the pilot's compartment of her steam-loader, Sally Chu smiled. Why? Because the six-armed freak heading her way had absolutely no idea what he was about to dally with here. None whatsoever. Okay, sure, from the outside, Sally's cherished robot exo-skeleton may not have looked much— dented, scuffed, crisscrossed with the lumpy steel scar tissue of countless welding repairs, and at least three versions behind the current models— but where it counted, the venerable machine was, in the not-so-humble opinion of Sally herself, one steam-powered, ass-kicking weapon of mass destruction. Modified and upgraded by Jess to

Sally's own specifications, these days the loader truly felt like an extension of Sal's body, and when she raised the control gauntlets now, clenching them into fists, a familiar thrill surged through her as the massive steel dukes of the loader itself mirrored her actions with effortless precision.

Seconds out then, as the fella in the bowtie said…

Eyes still fixed on the gun-toting blackhat heading her way, Sally barked out an order to Vera and Miss Lacey: "Go! Get Sissy!"

And go they did, ducking swiftly under the flatbed, then scurrying through to the opposite side of the train, out of Slinger's line of fire.

Inside the loader, Sally took a single step to the left, her robot exo-skeleton mimicking flawlessly and moving in to shield both Jess and Dave as the duo's angle grinders began to cut through the network of chains holding Momma to the wagon.

"So, *train robbing* now, huh?" Slinger called out as he stomped closer, all six of his weapons raised high. "You realize this means I can legally shoot every one of you on the spot."

Sally rolled her eyes and curled a lip. "Know what, bud? We got a saying where I come from. Goes something like this: *Screw you, motherhumper!*" and heels pounding the walk controls at her feet, Sally launched the loader at Slinger, slug after slug ricocheting off its bulletproof windshield as her opponent unleashed the lead in response. "Okay, sure, ain't exactly Shakespeare," Sally conceded. "Guess that dude mighta stuck a 'forsooth' in there or some such. Still, gets the job done, am I right?" with which words a swinging steel robo-fist smacked into the six-armed scumbag and sent him hurtling backwards.

But even mid-air the frickin blackhat managed to get off a shot. And a well-aimed one at that, the round slamming dead center into the steam-loader's front windshield, where somehow it managed to spiderweb the five-centimeter-thick armored glass panel.

Sally stifled a gasp. So much for 'bulletproof'.

Lurching forward, she stamped a robo-foot down at her scowling foe, now on his back on the rocky red ground. But against all odds the rat managed to roll clear, take aim, fire again.

And another hit, once again dead center of the windshield, the cracks there spreading wider.

"Oh, ffffforsooth," Sally muttered, shooting a glance at her rearview to take in the hunched backs of Jess and Dave, sparks flying all around the pair as they pressed their howling angle grinders into the fat metal links of Momma's chains...

●●●

Leaping down from the show train's passenger car, Vera landed in time to see Miss Lacey make a similar exit from the next car along.

180

Unfortunately, the look on the old woman's face once again told all: Sissy was *not* inside. Same as the carriage Vera herself had just searched. Same as the four carriages they'd searched before that. There was simply no sign of the creature anywhere. Or the rest of the tribe for that matter. Just car after car of bewildered, frightened show people.

"Dammit, where *is* she?" Vera spat and was on the point of setting off again when, from the carriage adjoining the one Miss Lacey had just exited, another figure suddenly emerged, jumping from the doorway to land trackside with a grunt. Vera recognized the man immediately—their old friend Vomit Beard—and took a step forward to question him. But before she could, the old monster hunter growled like a cornered animal, dodged past her, and then raced away.

"Hey!" Vera shouted after him, but the fellow was already gone, bolting for the muddy squalor of The Town With No Name opposite.

Shaking her head in frustration, Vera turned to Miss Lacey. "Come on. She's *got* to be here *somewhere*," and together the two of them took off once more, charging still farther up the show train.

•••

Time and again Sally rammed her robo-feet down

at the prone Slinger, but time and again the man simply rolled clear, the titanium-soled treads of Sal's steam-loader pounding uselessly into the rocky surface of Mars, kicking up ever more clouds of pale red dust.

Damn, but the guy was fast. *Crazy* fast. And did he ever even stop to take a breath? Did he hell. As robo-stomp after robo-stomp failed to connect with the grinning blackhat, round after round from the guy's six revolvers continued to smash into the windshield of Sally's loader, the cracks there spreading wider with every impact.

In her rearview, Sally once again caught the briefest glimpse of Jess and Dave, their angle grinders *still* pressed into the chains binding Momma to the flatbed, sparks *still* flying as the power tools did their fiery work.

Just what the hell was taking them so *long?*

Then BANG!—yet another slug hit the steam-loader's front windshield dead center, and this time the density of the cracks there seemed to increase a hundred-fold all at once, the entire armored glass panel turning milky-white in an instant, almost completely opaque.

Great. Just great. And now Sally could barely see a frickin thing…

25

Round Two

Hauling open the door to yet another of the show train's crew cars, Vera's eyes widened at the unexpected dazzle of a plush red and gold interior, and behind her, spotting that same flashy opulence as she hurried for the next car along, Miss Lacey stumbled to a halt then backed up a step.

"Zora," the old woman said, her voice husky with fury. "I'll handle this," and barging past Vera, Miss Lacey pulled herself up into the carriage doorway and stormed on in.

Heart thudding, Vera followed, stepping into the car to see the imposing figure of Zora Petrovna halfway down its main cabin. With her head stuck out an open window, the woman stood peering back towards the rear of the train, engrossed in whatever might be happening out there. Sally kicking Slinger's despicable backside, Vera fervently hoped, although the cacophony of gunshots and ricochets from that direction seemed to suggest that the owner of said backside was not going down without a significant fight.

Far from whirling in shock at the abrupt entrance of her two angry visitors, Zora continued for a moment to absorb the view at the rear of the train, before stepping back from the window and, with no discernible sense of urgency whatsoever, turning to Miss Lacey. "Annie," she said.

"Where is she?" Miss Lacey demanded, both her fists clenched tight, as if she might actually take a swing at Zora herself with her gnarled, old-lady knitting hands. "Where is Sissy? And where are the rest of the tribe?"

Zora's entirely unruffled response was to drop into the nearest satin-upholstered seat, set her booted feet up on the chair opposite, and flash Miss Lacey the kind of smile that made Vera want to employ language of which her parents would strongly have disapproved.

"Oh, please," Zora said. "You really think I'm interested in Sissy *now?* Or *any* of the rest of the tribe come to that. You've seen what we've got

184

here. That creature? Can you *imagine* what people will pay to see *her*? Annie, please, you're the best business manager this show ever had," and removing her boots from the chair opposite, Zora took a moment to dust and adjust the seat's plump cushion, before shoving the whole thing a centimeter or two in Miss Lacey's direction. "Come back, Annie. Please. Let's run with this together. We can even—"

The bang of an opening door interrupted, and whirling with Miss Lacey, Vera took a startled step back as a denim-clad figure stumbled through the entrance at the far end of the carriage. Though the man himself was unknown to her, his soiled and rumpled overalls suggested to Vera a member of the show train's locomotive crew. And from the look on his face, not an altogether happy member.

"Okay, Zora," the crewman said, "just what in the name of god almighty is going on *now*?"

Zora scowled back at the new arrival and opened her mouth to answer, but before she could, a nearby window exploded in a shower of glass fragments, and a bullet zinged through the carriage, cratering a wooden wall panel opposite in a follow-on shower of splinters.

Everyone dropped to the floor for cover. Well, everyone but Zora, who moved not a muscle and continued simply to scowl at the terrified crewman, now cowering beneath a table. "Do you mind, Joe? We're having a business meeting here."

Disbelief surged into the fellow's face. "Are you frickin *serious?*"

"*Excuse* me?"

"Okay, look, Zora, me and the turns, we been mulling things over," upon which another stray bullet came whining through the carriage to shatter a gaslight fitting directly above the unhappy crew member's head. Glass rained down on the terrified man, and after shaking the shards from his hair, he looked up again at his boss, a scowl now darkening *his* face.

"Zora, we need to talk," the man called Joe said, before turning to address Miss Lacey as well, the old woman now huddled with Vera in a corner. "Annie, you might wanna stick around and hear this too…"

● ● ●

Through the whited-out glass of her cracked windshield, Sally could see almost nothing, dim shapes at best, the most prominent among them being the huge rock pedestal that her adversary— the one she'd so gravely underestimated—had just dived behind for cover. Towering over the craggy outcrop in her steam-loader, Sally could hear the blackhat behind it—the click of gun cylinders sprung open then snapped shut.

The guy was reloading, and fast.

186

Not good.

"Hiding under rocks now, huh, Slinger?" Sally taunted. "Family gathering, right?"

Another click. Another snap. Then a sneered reply: "Ya got a smart mouth, kid. Gonna be a pleasure to close it. For good," and faster than a rattler on speed, the six-armed freak leapt into the open once more, all guns blazing.

Multiple impacts on her compromised windshield sent Sally staggering backwards in her loader, until at last, with a BANG like a cannon shot, the entire armored glass panel protecting Sal from Slinger's onslaught shattered into a million fragments and dropped away.

But that wasn't the worst.

At the very same instant, one of those same bullets must *also* have pierced a critical hydraulics cable in the machine's now unprotected cab, because Sally felt warm fluid splash down onto her shoulder, and all at once the entire steam-loader ground to a halt. Cursing furiously, Sally stamped the walk pedals at her feet, wrenched at the control gauntlets, but nothing. The loader was out. Kaput. Just three all-metal tons of dead frickin weight.

By the feet of the immobilized robo-suit, just meters away, Slinger grinned up at Sally, lingering with delight on her denim-clad frame, now fully exposed in the pilot's seat of the lifeless mech.

"Oh yeah," the blackhat drawled, "a *real* pleasure," and holstering all but one of his weapons, Slinger raised the remaining revolver, took the laziest of aims at Sally's forehead, and squeezed the trigger.

26

TKO

To say Slinger never saw it coming would, Jess imagined, be something of an understatement. Giant hairy fist slamming in stage right to send a fella sailing off in a blur of black denim and flailing limbs? Nope. Not a foreseeable way for *any* fight to end, let alone a mano-a-mecha affair like this one. As for the guy's final 'kill shot'? Almost as wide as the wide blue yonder that swallowed it up.

Even as Slinger's unconscious body thudded down nearly forty meters away, Momma, free of her chains at last, roared her triumph and beat at her gigantic chest, while at the same time, in the pilot's seat of her immobile steam-loader, Sally

189

slumped in manifest relief and began to extricate herself from the controls.

For her own part, Jess took just the briefest of moments to indulge the hot rush of victory, high-fiving Dave beside her, before turning to the sound of hurried footsteps.

Vera.

"Please tell me you found Sissy," Jess said as the English gal skidded to a stop in front of her.

"I'm afraid not," Vera answered. "Apparently they didn't take her."

"*What?*" Sally barked, jumping down from her dead steam-loader to join them.

"And they didn't take the rest of the tribe, either."

Jess scowled. "So where the hell *are* they all?"

Vera never got the chance to answer, because just then, another gunshot rang out, and with a communal gasp of shock, Jess and the others whirled to see the bartender of the Rusty Machete standing on the porch of the decrepit saloon, a smoking rifle pressed to his shoulder.

"I warned you, girlie," the bartender said, the barrel of his weapon leveled at Jess. "I *told* you, told you *all,* to get the hell gone. Couldn't have been clearer, I reckon. But nope, ya just didn't listen, did ya? Now, do I actually *want* to shoot a buncha teenagers in cold blood? No, I do not. I got me morals. Or ethics. Or some such Shinola.

Other folks round here though? Not so much," upon which, from what looked like pretty much every other building in the whole damn place, people began to step. People by the dozen. The entire profoundly unwashed population of The Town With No Name, it seemed like to Jess. And every single one of them armed to those broken and rotting back teeth.

In fewer than ten seconds, Jess, her crew, and Momma were surrounded, a hundred or more assorted firearms trained squarely on them, ready to deal death. And just when Jess thought things couldn't get any worse, a final figure came stumbling from the Rusty Machete.

Vomit Beard.

The grime-encrusted old hunter was armed too, Jess saw, though the rifle slung over *his* shoulder looked different somehow—a bizarre, oversized affair with a single fat barrel.

Beside Jess, Sally glowered. "Okay, not good. That's a high-power tranquilizer gun."

Jess glanced up at Momma, then back over at Vomit Beard, before returning her gaze to the bartender. "He's not taking her."

In response, the bartender cocked his rifle, and a hundred or more weapons followed suit in a sinister Mexican wave of *clunk-shucks*. "You took something of his, girlie. Fella got every right. Ethics, see?"

From the corner of one eye, Jess saw Vomit Beard load a massive dart into the tranquilizer gun.

"He's *not* taking her," Jess said again, fighting to keep her voice steady.

The bartender smiled. "Uh-huh. And who's gonna stop him?"

The answer to that turned out to be something *none* of them were expecting, not least the assembled residents of The Town With No Name.

From the hills beyond the filth-ridden settlement, an echoing cry suddenly rose up—a resonating animal roar that, to Jess, sounded strangely familiar. It was followed almost immediately by *further* roars—dozens of them, maybe even hundreds—and, after that, by a kind of sub-bass rumble that Jess detected as much through the soles of her boots as through her ears.

Then, just seconds later, cresting the low hills that surrounded The Town With No Name, the source of all these startling emanations came storming into view.

The missing tribe.

And in greater numbers than Jess had ever imagined could exist. *Far* greater. There seemed to be hundreds of the creatures, thundering towards the tiny town like a monstrous tsunami, howling their collective fury, shaking their clenched fists as they ran.

And at the head of this unlikely raiding party?

Sissy.

Still clad in the shredded remnants of Sally's show dress, and with Butch powering along at her shoulder, Miss Lacey's pride and joy led the entire terrifying charge, galloping full pelt for the filthy township, her howling cry—the one Jess had recognized—spurring on the legion of creatures in her wake.

All around, their weapons still raised, stunned townsfolk whirled to face the incoming monster army, and Jess heard a handful of gunshots ring out. But no more than that, because almost instantly, the entire population of The Town With No Name turned tail and began to run, fleeing for any of those surrounding hills not currently venting hairy monsters at them.

Mere seconds later, even as the last of the not-so-jolly villagers were still vacating the premises, Sissy, Butch, and the rest of the stampeding horde swarmed past the town perimeter to plow into the hopeless collection of rickety buildings that made up the squalid settlement.

And The Town With No Name quickly became The Town With No Future.

In a spiraling, shrieking fury, hairy fists began to pound at rotting timbers. Walls started to collapse, buildings to topple, crashing down around the marauding beasts in a storm of splinters and mud and flying hardware.

Roaring her own fury now, Momma took off, bounding away from Jess and her friends to join the howling throng, and half a dozen steps later she was stomping with the rest of them, building after building ground into the mud beneath her mighty feet.

Jess saw a smaller group of the beasts separate themselves from the main horde to descend upon the town square and the multitude of species still imprisoned there. Working together, this breakaway group quickly wrenched open or tore apart the cages holding all the other creatures, who, one by one, slithered, scuttled, or lurched away, vanishing into the surrounding chaos.

And through it all—transfixed by the entire shocking but oh-so-satisfying spectacle—Jess, Sally, Dave, and Vera could only stand and gape.

In less than a minute—*considerably* less, by Jess's reckoning—the greater part of The Town With No Name was little more than a jumble of broken timbers in a squelching sea of filth, with the last vestiges of its former population barely visible at all now, running for the hills beyond.

And even as the settlement's sole remaining upright structure—the Rusty Machete itself—crumbled into the mud beneath several hundred monstrous, stomping feet, Momma rose up to her full height once more and threw back her shaggy head, roaring her victory to the Martian heavens while she beat at her massive breast. Even on its own, it was a sound to inspire awe, but then, as the rest of the animals followed their leader's thunderous example, the effect grew more awesome still, building in wave upon wave until the very air itself trembled with the creatures' ecstatic triumph.

And at Momma's side, one creature in particular—the same one who might eventually take the grand matriarch's place—finally tore off the last remnants of Sally's show dress, pounded at her own not quite so massive breast, and roared along with them.

With Momma.

With the other creatures.

With her tribe.

27

Rom Com Finale

Only a little later, they were all of them, both humans and tribe, back safely at the creatures' treetop home, the Cannonball parked once more at the ancient science station's dilapidated platform, boiler steaming gently in the cool of the evening. A light rain had begun to fall, and with the Martian dusk now setting in proper, the sun crept towards the horizon through a wash of pastel purples while plaintive choruses of insect nightlife echoed softly through the branches of the giant tree.

In terms of setting an appropriate tone, Mars was doing a bang up job here, Jess thought, and as the inevitable 'goodbye scene' continued to play out before her, she felt the lump in her throat grow. Not that she was the only one thus afflicted. Next to her, Dave and Vera appeared similarly choked, while even Sally managed to look suitably somber.

As for the scene itself: in the greenery-tangled ruins of the mysterious lab, Miss Lacey stood facing a silent and downcast Sissy, while Momma, Butch, and the rest of the tribe looked on.

"I know you maybe don't do clothes anymore," Miss Lacey said to the young she-creature, "but humor me, yes?" and with tears brimming, the old lady draped a long woolen scarf—the one she'd been knitting since they'd set off—around Sissy's slumped shoulders, tying it tight as rain pattered down on them both. "Winter will be here before you know it," Miss Lacey continued, "and this place?" She looked about her with matronly disapproval. "Frankly, it could use a draft excluder or two."

Sissy glanced down at the scarf and up again, tears gathering in *her* eyes now too as she studied the small wilting figure before her. Then, moaning softly, the she-creature reached out and wrapped both arms tight around the old woman, hugging her with a fearsome intensity. Crushed in Sissy's powerful embrace, Miss Lacey struggled to get her next words out, but she got there in the end:

"And don't think I won't be visiting now and then either. You can't get rid of me that easily, I'm afraid."

From what Jess could see though, getting rid of Miss Lacey was about the farthest thing from Sissy's mind, because still the she-creature held on to the old woman, squeezing her tighter than ever.

"All right then," Miss Lacey said at last, "so, um… I suppose we'd best be getting on…" and with a motherly gentleness that sent a single tear rolling down Jess's own cheek, the old lady extricated herself from Sissy's arms then stepped back to rejoin the crew of the Cannonball.

For another long moment, Sissy just stood there, taking in each of the humans in turn, until at last, her dark eyes came to rest on Dave.

And there they lingered awhile…

… before darting uncertainly to Butch, standing in silence at Sissy's shoulder.

Once again, Sissy moaned softly…

… but then turned back to Dave and extended a single hairy claw. With the gesture, her moan became a low, aching whine, the message unmistakable:

Stay here. Stay with me.

Dave gulped, glancing first to Butch and then back to Sissy, finally meeting the she-creature's solemn gaze head on. "Hey, it's okay," he said to her. "You can go with him. It's cool. Really it is."

But no. Sissy stood firm, her soft whine growing more plaintive still, her single claw reaching for Dave, palm upwards, fingers extended.

"I mean it," Dave said to her, his words thickening with emotion. "Big strapping Chewbacca wannabe like that? Absolutely perfect for you. Seriously, girl. Perfect. Cos me? Ha! You could do better, know what I'm saying?"

But still Sissy made no move, her eyes fixed on the boy from Staines, her whine dropping almost to inaudibility.

Dave turned to the others. "Oh, god, I don't know what to—"

He never finished the sentence. Jess didn't let him. In retrospect, it *was* perhaps understandable that what Jess chose to do next would raise an eyebrow or two, but in her defense, it really *had* seemed to her the quickest, simplest, and most obvious solution at the time.

Stepping forward, Jess grabbed Dave by the shoulders, dragged him to her, and kissed him long and hard on the lips, before pulling away again and turning back to Sissy. "See? All good. You got your fella, I got mine. Romcom finale. We cool here?"

Dave—again, perhaps understandably—stood there in complete shock, while Sissy's eyes widened in surprise, her plaintive whine shut off with comic suddenness.

Eventually though, Sissy's extended claw dropped, and she moved towards Dave, stopping directly in front of him and Jess and contemplating them both with an entirely inscrutable blend of animal emotions. In truth, Jess wasn't at all convinced she wouldn't yet end up with a hairy fist in the face for her impudence. But no. Instead, Sissy threw her arms around Dave, crushing the poor guy in her ferocious embrace for several long seconds, before turning again and hurling herself at Butch behind her. With a room-shaking thud, the two creatures came slamming together, then just seconds later went tumbling through a doorway and out of view, fur flying, yelps of pleasurable excitement ringing out.

Such a moment was not, of course, one that Ms. Chu could let pass without comment. "I say again, *big hairy mirror,*" the gal drawled, flashing a vampish grin at Vera, who, true to her catholic schoolgirl form, managed nothing in response but a terrified gulp and a beetroot blush.

Meanwhile, Jess herself turned to a still dumbstruck Dave. "Sorry about that," she said. "Seemed like, you know, an obvious quick fix."

"Um… yeah," Dave replied. "Yeah, no worries…" and okay, even if there *was* just a hint of awkwardness in the exchange, well that was perfectly understandable, wasn't it? And certainly *not* something to support Vera's absurd theory of the previous evening—namely, that the fella had, in Vera-speak, *romantic aspirations* re Jess.

In plain ol' Jess-speak, *bull doo-doo*.

And anyway, it wasn't as if the guy was even Jess's type, right?

Like, *at all*.

"Okay then, folks," Jess said, snapping out of her musings and back into work mode, "so let's get the old gal fired up. Reckon we got one last job to do here. Sal, *you* are gonna like this…"

Not twenty minutes later, the Cannonball Express came roaring through the narrow pass in the crater that surrounded the giant tree, streaking away at speed. And as it did, two dazzling beams of electric blue erupted from the twin barrels of the loco's roof-mounted laser cannon. Aimed backwards and very slightly down, the beams—a continuous stream that managed to stay just above the roof of the train's rearmost wagon—slammed into the railroad behind, sending steel, timber, and significant quantities of Mars itself hurtling skyward in a thunderous and ongoing trail of destruction.

In the driver's cab of the Cannonball, Jess peered backwards through a side window to watch the show, while from the gunner's seat above, Sally's whoops of vandalous delight rang out, audible even over the roar of the loco and the continuous boom of the explosions behind them.

Jess smiled, a dark satisfaction rising in her heart. Okay, sure, determined and unscrupulous people might still be able to get to these 'hunting grounds' via other means, but this should at least stop the bulk of the traffic. And hey, who knew, maybe with the razing of The Town With No Name, business here was done for good.

They could at least hope so.

Turning front once more, Jess eased the throttle back a notch and let the rhythmic clatter of wheels on track calm her thoughts as the Cannonball Express steamed onward for home.

28

For the Sake of Science and Stuff

Seriously, Levi Zabulon Slinger thought, that Wile E. Coyote fella did *not* know how lucky he was. No way, no how. One quick plummet into a yawning canyon, one donut-shaped puff of smoke, and at least the hapless toon had some kind of closure.

But *this?*

Tramping onward through the relentless rainstorm, Slinger glanced down at the mud-drenched map in his hand, before looking up again into the contemptuous countenance of surely his greatest mistake. Still trudging along by his side, the ex-boss of Mars's foremost traveling carnival, and ex-wife of Mars's foremost six-armed gunslinger, continued to await an answer to the question she'd just posed, her face like proverbial thunder. Indeed, being currently in a position to compare and contrast with the real thing, Slinger had only recently concluded that *actual* thunder was significantly more appealing, and significantly *less* threatening. As things stood, the idea that a pair of lightning bolts might yet emerge from Zora Petrovna's seething black eyes seemed not entirely beyond the bounds of possibility.

"Dunno what else to tell you," Slinger said at last. "Cartography don't lie, Zora. Nearest settlement, sixty-three kilometers this-a-way," and he jabbed twice with a forefinger, first at the map in his other hand, then at the bleak expanse of muddy red wasteland that stretched ahead.

The woman came back with a dark grimace, her eyes—apparently lacking integrated lightning bolts after all—shifting to ponder the lonely stretch of single track railroad she and Slinger trailed along beside. "And the chances of us hitching a ride from out here?" she asked—

—upon which cue a familiar red locomotive roared past, twin blasts from its roof-mounted laser cannon blowing the railroad to smithereens.

Slinger sighed as debris rained down around them both. "Slim," he replied.

• • •

"Oh, come on, gimme *something* here," Sally moaned at Jess. "*Anything!*"

Poised at the throttle of the speeding Cannonball, Sally beside her shoveling coal, Jess rolled her eyes and wondered for the umpteenth time just what the big deal was here. "For Pete's sake," she said to her annoyingly persistent friend, "how many ways can I say this, Sal? It was a *fake kiss*. An *act*. Dave knows that, you know that, *everybody* knows that."

"Whatever. Still need details, babe. Moisture factor: dry or smooshy? Dental engagement: none, glancing, a danger to enamel? These things need to be recorded, hon. For the sake of, like, science and stuff."

"And not cos you get off on them?"

"So I'm horny for science. Sue me."

Jess huffed out an exasperated sigh. In fairness to Sal, the first leg of their return journey—back to the ruins of The Town With No Name—really hadn't been so bad. There they had dropped off Miss Lacey at the waiting show train, before wishing the old lady well and saying their final goodbyes. All fine and dandy. But after that— once the Cannonball had set off for home proper—that was when Sally's nagging had *truly* begun, remaining essentially relentless ever since.

205

And they weren't even halfway home yet.

"You're really not gonna let this go, are you?" Jess said to her friend.

"Just one frickin word, babe. One. Then I'll shut up, I swear," and crossing her heart in the time-honored playground fashion, Sally set aside her fireman's shovel and stood there in silent, solemn-faced anticipation.

Stifling a further sigh, Jess thought for a long moment. "Okay," she said eventually, "it was… nice. Happy now?"

"*Nice?*"

"Yes. *Fake* but… *nice.*"

A long pause followed.

Well, not *that* long actually.

"So let's define *fake*. Do you mean *fake* as in— Ow ow *ow!* Did you *seriously* just Chinese burn me? You know that's racist, right?"—

—and turning front again, Jess gave in to a surreptitious smile then hauled back on the throttle, feeling the Cannonball's engine surge beneath her as the loco began to pick up speed, carrying its weary crew homeward once more.

29

Prince Valiant

From the open windows of the Lucky Horseshoe Saloon, the easy rhythms of a foxtrot skipped their way out into the Martian night, the sultry voice of Sally 'The Rose of Tranquility' Chu imbuing the song's cutesy lyric with a sensuality it didn't quite deserve:

> *"One is dashing and oh-so-bold.*
> *One is sweet with a heart of gold.*
> *Oh, Momma, what's a girlie to do?"*

But hey, that was Sally for you, Vera Middleton thought, always with the steamy stuff, following which rumination Vera allowed herself a single wistful sigh… before hastily refocusing on the matter in hand. Or, in this case, in *arms*.

Dave, of course.

Currently foxtrotting with her in the shadows around the side of the packed saloon, their refugee from a twenty-first century Earth was actually doing rather well tonight, Vera thought. *Very* well, in fact. Assured, nimble, graceful. So far all of Vera's toes had remained more or less intact. On top of which, the lad seemed to have scrubbed up rather nicely too, what with his smart jacket and shiny shoes and snazzy new necktie. If not dressed to kill, Vera reflected, then at least dressed to give something a jolly good biffing.

"You know what?" Vera said as Dave executed a neat and accurate promenade. "I'm beginning to think this Prince Charming Gambit of yours might *actually* pay off."

As ever with these teasing inferences of Vera's, Dave chose only to frown back in stark defiance. "For the last time," he said, "I *ain't* doing any of this to impress *Jess*. I only want to…" but then his voice tailed off, his dancing feet following a moment later. For several seconds more, Dave stood there chewing on his lower lip, before finally he gave in to a sigh and shot Vera a look tinged with just the merest glimmer of hope. "You really think so?"

Ha! At *last,* Vera thought, cheering inwardly. "Oh, golly, yes," she chirped, determined now not to make a big thing of what had clearly been a difficult admission for the lad. "Between me and Sissy, I think we have turned out a pretty natty mover, I truly do," and stepping backwards, Vera proceeded to subject Dave to a bout of stern maternal scrutiny, straightening his tie, brushing down the shoulders of his jacket, then offering a final nod of approval. "So *go*," she said, indicating the saloon's side door. "*Now!* Just get in there and, you know—" Vera raised a hand to shoulder level, palm forward, fingers separated, two one side, two the other. A 'Vulcan salute' in Daveworld, Vera was rather pleased with herself to recall. "May the force be with you," she added, still more pleased to remember the gesture's accompanying salutation.

Dave opened his mouth as if to say something but seemed to think better of it and instead leaned forward, kissed Vera on the cheek, then turned to face the saloon. Back straight, chin forward, the boy drew in a deep breath, flexed his shoulder muscles, and declared, "Okay then, I am *going.*"

"Boldly?"

"Is there any other way?" and with a final determined nod, the lad strode manfully forward into the merry bustle of the Lucky Horseshoe.

Smiling, Vera gave herself a mental pat on the

back then followed him through the door—

—just in time to watch Dave's manful stride take him thudding into the very object of his affections—Jess, gliding across the dancefloor in the arms of…

Ah, and *there* was a spanner in the works if ever Vera had seen one.

"Hey, Dave," Jess said, recovering. "Where've you been? Look who *finally* turned up!"

"Dave, my man," Declan Donavan said. "How goes it?"

Yes indeed.

Declan Donovan.

Leader of Mars's *Free Air* rebel group, would-be hero of the masses, and caretaker of New Avalon, the mysterious underground eco-system Jess and her crew had encountered on their very first outing in the Cannonball. Also, Vera would be forced to concede, one super-handsome and self-assured son-of-a-wotsit.

For tonight's prospective Prince Charming, this would *not*, Vera imagined, be seen as the happiest turn of events, and instantly validating her concerns, Dave proceeded to sag visibly, croaking out a limp, "Hey, Declan," while Jess, entirely oblivious to Dave's discomfort, beamed up at the blue-eyed Irish Adonis still attached to her right arm.

"I was just telling Jess," Declan continued, "that

leaf sample you sent us—the one from the tree—it's a perfect genetic match for one of the main species in New Avalon. And I mean *perfect*. As soon as the results came in I just had to get over here, let you all know."

"Great," the drooping lump that was Dave from Staines managed, and still watching all from the saloon's open side door, Vera felt her heart go out to the lad.

"Don't you see?" Jess said to Dave. "The crater. Declan reckons a massive meteor impact must have broken the surface there eons ago. Exposed what lies *beneath* it."

"*Another* New Avalon," Declan continued. "*Gotta* be. We've always theorized that more must exist. We've been looking for them for years now. But this is the very first direct evidence to support the theory."

Jess took up the thread again: "The tree must have grown up from below, see? Through the cracks made by the meteor impact."

"Exactly," Declan said. "As for its unusual size, well, radiation *might* account for that, we're not too sure at the moment. Same goes for the creatures. Martian engineering or illegal gene tampering by the early settlers, we don't really know as yet. Either way though, this is *seriously* huge, know what I'm saying?"

Both Jess and Declan continued to beam at

Dave, who, to his credit, nodded back and finally succeeded in manufacturing a smile of his own.

Still beaming, Jess turned again to Declan. "But hey, enough talking shop, mister. We dancing here or what?"

"Yes, ma'am, we certainly are," and with that, the pair glided away into the crowd, leaving Dave to shore up his faltering smile while The Rose of Tranquility continued to wring salacious meaning from a 1920s song lyric:

> *"One likes tango-ing after dark.*
> *One likes strolling in Central Park.*
> *Oh, Momma, what's a girlie to do?"*

Eventually, Vera took a step forward and moved in by Dave's side, watching along with him as his eyes followed Jess and Declan's progress around the dancefloor.

"You do know Prince Charming was actually the boring one," Vera said at last, upon which remark Dave seemed finally to pull himself back into the Land of the Living.

"Huh?"

"I mean, what did the fellow even *do?* Throw fancy parties, dance a bit, get all mopey about some woman who lost her shoe," and taking Dave into hold again, Vera began to lead the fellow around the saloon's cramped and beer-sticky floor. "Other princes were always *much* better," Vera continued as they danced. "You know, the ones who... oh, I don't know... who stood up to the baddies when it looked like no one else would. The ones who saved princesses from their evil captors. The ones who fought to make the world a better place. For everyone... and for every*thing*." Pausing mid-step, Vera turned just a little so that Dave could take in the colorful poster pinned to the saloon wall behind her:

COMING SOON!
LACEY'S CARNIVAL OF MARS
NOW ENTIRELY CREATURE FREE!

At last, Dave spoke again: "Hey, you're right! Maybe I should try doing some of *that* stuff instead."

It was Vera's turn to sag. "Please tell me you're—"

Dave rolled his eyes—of *course* he was kidding—and after a final glance across the dancefloor at Jess and Declan, he hoisted himself straight once more. "Come on then," he said. "Bit more practice ain't gonna hurt, right? Next song, I am *absolutely* asking Jess up."

Vera smiled, and off they stepped once more, Dave actually *leading* this time. Good lad.

"And Vera..."

"Yes?"

"Thanks."

"Oh, Dave, you are very wel—OW!"

"Sorry…"

•••

So hey, the big Irish fella could foxtrot too, Jess thought, casting an admiring eye over the tall blonde specimen currently leading her around the dancefloor. Good to know. *Very* good, in fact. Of course, exactly why the guy had taken so long to get back in touch with her after seeming so keen before… well, that was a matter for another time perhaps. Or maybe even for never. Cos seriously, if this fella turned out *not* to be interested in Jess after all, then hoo-boy did her internal sensors need some *radical* recalibrating!

In the corner of the saloon, the band eased its way into a moody instrumental section, and as it did so, the sight of something over Declan's shoulder drew Jess's eye—Dave dancing with Vera. Jess smiled. And it wasn't a smile of amusement either. More like respect. Because from what Jess could see, Dave really did seem to have come on apace with his foxtrot, certainly since Jess's feet had last suffered beneath those hefty size tens. Guy was *looking* rather smart too, she noted, before wondering (not for the first time tonight) why somehow she seemed to have

214

exchanged barely a dozen words with Dave this entire week, and most of *those* about a minute ago. Was he still feeling awkward about the fake kiss thing? Surely not. Either way, maybe it was time to get that whole business behind them for good. Because, weirdly, Jess had kinda been missing the fella's incessant and obscure nerd-talk. Go figure, huh?

So, decision made then. The very next dance, Our Dave it would be.

And as the band in the corner concluded its instrumental break, Sally's sultry tones emerged once more to slink their way through the none too fragrant air of the Lucky Horseshoe:

> *"One a scoundrel and one a brick,*
> *Lousing up the arithmetic,*
> *Cos one and one and one can never make two.*
> *And oh, Momma, what's a girlie to do?"*

THE END

of

CANNONBALL EXPRESS: *Hellbeast of Mars*

But Jess and her crew return

in…

Order it now at the following link:

getbook.at/trainrobbersofmars

And if you've enjoyed *this* book, please consider leaving an Amazon review or star rating. Big name publishers have millions to spend on advertising, but independently published books like the CANNONBALL EXPRESS series rely largely on reader recommendations. Because of this, an Amazon review (even just a couple of words) or simple star rating can be a massive help.

•••

WANNA STAY UP TO SPEED ON THE CANNONBALL EXPRESS?

There are millions of books on Amazon, and we're thrilled you found this one. But if you'd like to know when the *next* CANNONBALL EXPRESS book comes out, instead of leaving it to chance, join the Kit Kane mailing list, and we'll email you on release day.

Yes please! – kitkane.com/join

No thanks, I'll take my chances.

Or to get CANNONBALL EXPRESS updates via your favorite online platform, you can follow Kit on Amazon, Facebook, Goodreads, and others. Use the link below for further details:

kitkane.com/follow

ABOUT THE AUTHOR

Under a different name, Kit Kane has spent the last twenty years writing comedy, drama, and animation for UK television, contributing scripts to many globally acclaimed series, including Academy Award-winning productions from Aardman Animation and the BBC.

Printed in Great Britain
by Amazon